Rescuing RILEY

S.B. ALEXANDER

Cover copyright © 2024 by S.B. Alexander
Photography by: Furios Fotog
Model: Brent Whitaker

Rescuing Riley

First Edition: September 2018

E-book ISBN-13: 978-1-954888-54-8
Paperback Print ISBN-13: 978-1-954888-55-5

1

RILEY

I walked out of the Sacramento airport and into an oven. The temperature had to be a hundred degrees or more, and even though I didn't feel an ounce of humidity like I usually did in Boston, I felt as though I were suffocating.

On the flip side, I also felt free for the first time in over a month. I'd shut myself off from the rest of the world to brood over a breakup that had hit me right between the eyes. I was madder at myself than I was at the jerk I'd thought wanted a serious relationship—mad because I hadn't seen the forest for the trees. I was usually in tune to the signs. After all, my dad had cheated on my mom. But I'd been so preoccupied with my job that I hadn't been focused on my relationship. My job as a wedding planner kept me busy, especially the month before a client's wedding.

Regardless, my ex, John, and I had never exchanged the word "love." We'd never expressed our feelings to one another. I couldn't say I loved him. My best friend Liza had said my ego was shattered. Maybe so. But I did like John a lot. He had a big heart. He had a great job as a sales rep for a technology company, and he'd treated me well.

Outside Sacramento Airport, the people around me were in a

hurry, darting around others who were hugging loved ones, or dumping their suitcases into cars before they drove off.

I texted Liza to let her know I was standing outside baggage claim. The last time we talked, which was the night before, she'd told me she would be waiting in the cell phone lot.

Cars slowed to a crawl, and drivers scanned the crowd around me for their guests.

I waited for the ping, alerting me to a text from Liza, but there was nothing, not even the three dots that indicated someone was typing.

Suddenly, I got an eerie chill, as though something bad was about to happen, but I shook it off. The plane had landed a few minutes early, and I'd told Liza to give me thirty minutes after I got off the plane to get my luggage.

I navigated through the waiting passengers and found a quiet spot at the end of the glass building, near the taxicab stands to lean against. Then I sent Liza another text to let her know where I was. While I waited, I people-watched, which was something I loved to do. A mom scolded her five-year-old son. A businessman typed on his phone. And two lovers embraced.

I sighed. John and I had done that very thing when he'd returned after a week on the road. I missed feeling a man's arms around me, giving me that sense that someone cared for me in an intimate way.

But as my brother, Ross, kept telling me, "John was never going to get serious with you."

Again, I was mad at myself for not seeing the signs. Some of his actions should've clued me in. Granted, he traveled around the country for his job. Showing up late for our date or cancelling on me at the last minute because of a delayed or missed flight wasn't unheard of. But toward the end, his excuses had piled up until I confronted him. When I did, he caved, spilling his guts on how he was seeing another woman who lived in Chicago.

Thinking about that still stung. Liza had recommended that I get away from the fast pace of Boston and my job. I'd debated long and hard. As a wedding planner, my job was nonstop most of the year, but busier than ever from May to September. But that August, I had only two clients getting married. Otherwise, I wouldn't have been sweating in over a hundred-degree heat, although I had two awesome assistants who could handle the big day for one of my clients while I was away.

Besides, the last time I'd seen my BFF was over a year ago when she was boarding a plane to move back to Northern California. I missed her terribly. We talked once a week since she'd left, but as of late, she'd been checking on me since my breakup.

Our plans were to kick back and see the sights of NorCal, maybe tour a winery or two, and visit Redwood Cove. Liza had mentioned there was a ton to do in the quaint town, like whale watching, great sea life, and zip lining if I was into that. But I wasn't one for heights, testing my fate on a thin line, and flying at high speeds over some ravine or canyon or whatever. I didn't even like roller coasters. I'd been traumatized once when I was a little girl, and since then, no one could coax me onto one; even peer pressure didn't work.

Nevertheless, I couldn't wait to wrap my arms around Liza. I couldn't wait to talk into the wee hours of the morning and hear all about her job at a top-notch fashion company in San Francisco—Stitches Inc. She hardly talked about her job on the phone, although when she did, it was about some new design she was working on and a fashion show or two.

I was happy for her. When she'd lived in Boston, she worked for a fashion company that was eventually raided by the FBI. Her employer was one of the prominent mafia families in Boston. Liza hadn't known that when she'd gotten hired, and she'd told the FBI that she had never seen anything illegal.

After the raid, she'd quit and searched for another job for months. Every company she'd interviewed with had been frank with her, saying, "You worked for one of the largest mafia families in the New England area. We don't want trouble."

She'd decided to spread her wings and look at companies around the country, concentrating on San Francisco. Most of her family lived in the NorCal area, but she wasn't exactly close to her dad. However, she was tight with her cousin Josh, who I hadn't met yet.

Anyway, since I'd made the decision to come two weeks ago, the airlines didn't have many flights available to choose from among the airports in the NorCal area. So I had to settle on Sacramento and fly out on Thursday instead of Friday like I'd wanted to. Besides, Fridays were a busy day for travel. John had always complained about how airports were packed and flights were overbooked on Fridays.

A taxicab driver wearing a San Francisco Giants ball cap came up to me. "Do you need a ride?"

The baggage claim area was thinning out, and the sun was dipping behind the three-story parking garage across from me.

"No, thank you," I said. "I'm waiting on my ride."

He quietly went back to his cab adjacent to me.

I called Liza, and the line went straight to voice mail. *Odd.*

As long as I'd known Liza, she wasn't the type to be late. That eerie feeling I'd gotten earlier came back with a vengeance. I didn't have a backup plan, although I could get a rental car easily. In fact, I'd suggested to her that I would do just that, but she'd insisted on picking me up. "The drive will give us more time to catch up," she'd said.

Don't panic. She's twenty minutes late. She'll show up.

Someone coughed as they walked past me, snapping me back to the present and making me shed some of the cold chill that seemed to be seeping into my veins.

I peeked around the building for no other reason than to take a breath and tell myself nothing had happened to Liza.

Blood orange colored the horizon in the distance.

My off-the-shoulder blouse was starting to stick to me as the sweat trickled down my back and stomach. It was time to go back into the air-conditioned building while I decided on my next move.

Once inside, the aroma of coffee hit me, and my taste buds perked up. Suddenly, my body was starting to feel the three-hour time change.

My phone rang as I was about to get in line for some much-needed caffeine. I answered it without looking at the screen. "Liza, where are you?"

"Sis," my brother, Ross, said. "You sound panicked. What's going on?"

My twin brother knew me sometimes better than I knew myself, although it wasn't hard to detect the hitch in my voice.

I slid over to a quiet spot near the elevator. "I can't get ahold of Liza. She's late. Like thirty minutes late now."

"I knew I should've come with you," he said.

"I'm a big girl." I tried to fill my tone with confidence, but with the panic coursing through me, I was failing badly.

One of my flaws was that I jumped to conclusions too quickly and immediately thought the worst. I couldn't help it, though. I had grown up in a rough neighborhood, with a cheating dad, then a single mom after she had kicked out my cheating dad. Plus, our house had been robbed several times. Looking over my shoulder had become the norm, especially when Ross wasn't with me.

"Besides, I'm on a girls' trip with my bestie. No men allowed."

"What are you going to do, then?" Ross asked.

"I'm going to call her office first, and if I strike out, then her cousin Josh."

"You mean the ex-Navy SEAL?" Ross asked a little excitedly.

My brother was into military and war movies. He even loved to watch those programs on how Navy SEALs train. He'd wanted to go into the military but had decided against it when Mom and Dad had gotten a divorce. Ross hadn't wanted to leave Mom and me alone.

My phone alerted me to an incoming call from a number I didn't recognize. "Hold on. This might be Liza now." I switched over to answer.

"Hi, Riley. I'm Taylor, Liza's assistant. She's stuck in a meeting with an important client. Is there any way you can rent a car and head to her cousin's bed and breakfast in Redwood Cove? I'll text you the address. She also said she would call as soon as she can."

I guess I was renting a car after all. "I'm supposed to stay with her at her apartment. I can meet her there."

"No. She insisted that you head to Redwood Cove Inn. It's going to be a late night for her."

A bed and breakfast sounded so much better than an apartment in the city anyway. "Okay, but have her call me as soon as she can, though."

"I will." Then the line went dead.

I switched back to Ross. "Liza got stuck at work. I'm going to rent a car and make my way to Josh's in Redwood Cove. I'll check in with you when I get there."

"You better. Or I'm taking the next flight out."

I laughed, even though he was serious. He'd always been so protective of Mom and me.

"I have my mace if that makes you feel better." Mace wouldn't completely stop an attacker, but it would slow someone down, allowing me time to get away.

"Call me as soon as you get there," he said. "Do you hear me?"

"Loud and clear." I hung up before he could give me his speech on "Make sure you look at what's around you. Don't forget to use the mace and knee them in the groin if you have to."

While I was a confident woman, I was a little leery about finding my way to Redwood Cove. Not because of getting attacked, but because darkness would set in soon, and I wasn't a great nighttime driver.

2

JOSH

I rubbed my temples, wanting nothing more than to take a walk on the beach with my dog, Charlie, and throw the ball while he ran and I walked along the shore, or even take him to the dog park not far from the water. But that would have to wait. The inn my parents owned was slammed for a Thursday, with guests checking in. Normally, I didn't help out much at the front desk, mainly because I could hardly hear, which was a problem since a conversation between a guest and me was important during the check-in process.

But with one of my employees off for a couple of days, I had to help out.

Still, the place was overbooked. August was always a high time for us. People were on vacation, kids were out of school, and my guess was that families saved their trips until the week or two before school started.

Charlie nudged me with his wet nose. I looked down as he went over to the door. We had a bell to alert us of incoming guests, and he always pointed out where the noise was coming from.

Drake, one of my employees and a good friend, was working the desk. He leaned over and spoke into my right ear, which was my good ear, although good for me meant I could only hear if a person was close to me or talked loudly. My other ear hadn't been so lucky, thanks to a military mission gone wrong.

"Maybe you should head back to your office. I got this."

I chuckled as I scanned the lobby full of guests waiting in line to get their room. "I'm good."

He shook his head. "Liza picked the wrong week to go have fun."

"You mean Elliot chose the wrong time to take a vacation," I fired back. As the manager, I had the option of not approving Elliot's vacation, but he was taking his daughter to college on the other side of the country. I couldn't say no. I believed family always came first. Still, Liza liked to help out when she could.

Drake smoothed a hand over his bald head. "You're right. But I like Liza working with me."

I cocked an eyebrow, detecting that maybe the recent divorcee was into my cousin, which was a surprise to me, although I didn't pay attention to the flirtatious actions of others like Drake did.

Charlie returned, escorting a gray-haired woman up to the counter. Or rather, he walked alongside her as though he were protecting her.

I circled the front desk to greet the old lady and help her with her luggage. First, I bent down and scratched Charlie's beard. "Good boy." Then I rose. "Can I take your luggage while you check in?" If Drake wanted to handle the desk on his own, then I could help with luggage.

It was best I did anyway, since my hearing was crap. The doctors had said hearing aids wouldn't help me, and I'd been to several specialists since being discharged from the Navy.

She gave me a warm smile, then her lips started moving. I was a good lip reader. I'd mainly learned that technique in one of my many missions as a Navy SEAL way before I lost my hearing. Sometimes, I thought fate had been preparing me for what was to come.

I turned so my right ear was facing my elderly guest. "Can you repeat that?" I leaned in a tad so my good ear was closer to her. If the drone of the other voices around us were quieter or nonexistent, then I would've been able to make out what she'd said. "I'm hearing impaired."

She slapped a hand over her heart before she started signing.

I'd only been home a year from my mission in Afghanistan, and I was slowly getting acclimated to sign language. She signed that she was sorry.

I nodded as I made the gesture for thank you.

I checked on Drake, and he was still busy with a guest. "Can I have your credit card? I'll get you all set up for your room."

She made quick work of getting me her card, which read Janet Stone.

"Ms. Stone, give me a few minutes, and I'll have your room key for you. Charlie, stay here."

Charlie sat at Janet's feet, and within five minutes, I returned to the woman's side and handed her a room key. Then I held out my arm. "I'll escort you to the elevator."

Charlie popped up.

With my free hand, I grabbed the handle of Ms. Stone's roller back and pulled it as we headed away from the front desk.

"He sure is a pretty golden retriever. My grandson is in need of a service dog; actually, a therapy dog. He's been diagnosed with PTSD from an accident he was in. Where did you get Charlie?"

"A local breeder named Carol Graves. I'll be sure to give you her contact information."

"Thank you so much. Maybe I could visit her while I'm here," she said.

We were just approaching the elevator when my dad powered out of the office in his wheelchair. He regarded Janet with a tinge of surprise swimming in his green eyes.

I stopped mid-stride. "Dad, I thought you were taking a nap."

"I couldn't sleep. Mrs. Stone, it's good to see you again."

Pinching her eyebrows together, she let go of my arm and sized up my dad. "Oliver, what happened?"

I wasn't surprised Dad knew Janet. After all, he and Mom owned the inn. Dad had purchased the place after he'd retired from the army fifteen years ago.

He mashed his lips into a thin line as his hand hovered over the control on the wheelchair. "ALS." His tone was polite, but I could detect his anger over his predicament.

A week after my mom passed, Dad had started to slur his speech. Six months later, he'd been diagnosed with Amyotrophic Lateral Sclerosis or ALS. He still hadn't come to terms with the disease. I couldn't say that I had either. There was no cure for ALS, and each day, I watched my active, happy, and virile father go downhill, and it gutted me.

Once again, Janet touched her heart.

I petted Charlie's head. "I should get back to help Drake."

She gave me a hug. "Thank you for your sweet hospitality. Now I know where you get it from."

I did take after my dad in several ways. He'd always taught me to make sure the guests were well taken care of. After all, they paid the bills. But his morals went deeper than money. He loved to help people. He loved to chat them up. He loved that he could provide an escape for vacationers to have fun and unwind. More than all that, he'd always taught me to be polite to anyone no matter if it was a stranger or a returning guest walking into the inn.

I hugged Mrs. Stone back. Her rose scent reminded me of my mom, and suddenly I was trying to keep the tears at bay. Mom had passed eleven months prior from pancreatic cancer. So the pain was still etched in my mind.

Janet edged back. "Your son is handsome," she said to Dad.

"Like father, like son," Dad teased.

"For sure," Janet said. "I have to make a call. Afterwards, Oliver, would you like to get a coffee?"

My dad smiled. I couldn't remember the last time I'd seen him light up. "I would love that. Meet me in the restaurant." He pointed to the small eatery we had on the property.

My heart soared at seeing a spark in his eyes. I wanted nothing more than to see my dad walk again. But with no cure for ALS, I didn't see that happening. His muscles would continue to deteriorate, as would his diaphragm.

One day at a time, man. One day at a time.

I had to consistently repeat that motto. In addition to taking care of my dad, my current mission was to do everything I could to keep the inn running. Aside from that, nothing else mattered, although Dad kept egging me on to find a woman and settle down.

While that request did appeal to me, I was too busy to find a woman. Sure, as a man, I had needs. I'd seen a few beautiful ladies check in to the inn during the time I'd been home from the Navy. Some had been interested in having dinner with me, but none had made my heart skip a beat.

After Janet boarded the elevator, I said to Dad, "It's nice to see you smile. You should do that more."

"And you should find yourself a bride."

Charlie nudged my hand with his wet nose.

I looked around to see what noise he was alerting me to, but he wasn't running to show me where the noise was coming from.

The lobby had thinned out. Only one younger man was at the front desk, and Drake was handing him a room key. Everything seemed normal.

"So you agree with Dad," I said to Charlie.

He wagged his tail.

My phone vibrated in my jeans pocket, and my dad gave me a wave before he wheeled into the restaurant.

I dug my cell out of my pocket and lifted it to my good ear. "Liza, is everything okay?"

She should have been at the Sacramento airport, picking up her best friend. Both were scheduled to hang in Redwood Cove during one of the days Riley was visiting.

Liza had shown me a picture of Riley, and since then, I'd been dying to meet the pretty lady.

"I got caught at work, so I never made it to Sac. Riley is going to kill me."

"You left her hanging at the airport?"

Liza had talked about seeing her best friend nonstop for the last two weeks.

"I couldn't help it. My largest customer showed up madder than hell today. Anyway, I can't chat. I tried to call Riley, but she's not answering. Taylor talked to her earlier. Riley should be at your place soon. Can you entertain her and give her a room? I'll meet up with you guys tomorrow. It's going to be a late night here at the office."

I could detect fear in her voice. "Cousin, you sound off."

"Tired. That's all."

"Why don't I believe you?" I replied.

"Josh, please take care of Riley." She hung up before I could question her further.

She'd delivered the last sentence as though she would never see her friend again. I was tempted to call her back, but I knew she wouldn't tell me anything more than she already had.

I scratched my neck as I went over to Drake. "Do we have any rooms available?" I knew the answer but asked just the same in the hopes someone had canceled.

His brown eyes went wide as he shook his head. "You know we're booked solid through Monday."

I ran a hand through my sandy-blond hair. "Liza's friend needs a room tonight." I also hadn't gotten a chance to ask my cousin why Riley wasn't staying at her place in the city.

Charlie went over to his bed behind the counter and plopped down.

Drake waggled his dark eyebrows. "You mean the hot beauty we've seen pictures of?" Drake was recently divorced. He was a surfer dude with no kids and now played the field.

"The very one."

"She could stay at my place," Drake said.

I chuckled. "That isn't happening. She's not available anyway." I remembered Liza mentioning that Riley had a boyfriend.

I got on the computer. "I'll check the other hotels in the area." That way when she arrived, I could at least have a room for her somewhere. But the more I searched, the more I started to panic. Not one hotel within a thirty-mile radius had any openings. I wasn't surprised with the summer winding down and vacationers rushing to get the last-minute summer sun and activities in before school began.

I needed to think, and Charlie needed a bathroom break. So with the lobby still quiet, I said to Charlie, "Come on, boy."

I was headed out through the main entrance when the door opened.

All I saw at first were painted-red toenails peeking through high-heeled sandals. Then my gaze traveled up long legs until I locked eyes with a black-haired goddess.

Charlie nuzzled her hand as my jaw slackened.

She bent down and petted Charlie. "Hey there. What's your name?"

I tried to speak, but Riley had my tongue twisted. Her pictures didn't do her justice. Her long black hair had a blue tint to it, and her curves were... well, curvy. But what had my stomach doing somersaults were her light-gray eyes that reminded me of a cloudy day when rain threatened. I loved days like that when I could kick my feet up on the porch rail while sitting in a rocking chair, waiting for the clouds to open up.

"His name is Charlie," I finally said.

Climbing to her feet, Riley held out her hand.

The minute we shook, an electrical charge jolted me in a good way, even more so when she smiled and batted those luscious lashes that framed her blue-rimmed gray eyes.

I didn't believe in love at first sight, but maybe I should have. My body heated and reacted in ways I hadn't felt since Marybeth, my first love, in high school.

3

RILEY

I was exhausted as I walked into the Redwood Cove Inn. I swore I could've fallen on the flowered loveseat not too far off to my right. Instead, I swayed when I rose from petting Charlie, who seemed happy to see me, even though I didn't know the beautiful golden retriever.

The tall, muscled, and handsome man, who was ever the gentleman, steadied me.

I blushed as I laid eyes on him. When I did, butterflies took flight. Eyes as green as a lush forest regarded me.

"Josh, right?" I stammered out of my dry mouth.

I knew he was Liza's cousin. She'd texted me a picture or two every now and again of both of them lounging on the veranda that wrapped around the inn, overlooking the ocean. I was excited to see the place and even relax on the veranda while sipping cold lemonade, even though the weather in Redwood Cove wasn't as unbearably hot as it was in Sacramento.

He nodded, a clump of his thick sandy-blond hair falling forward. I was tempted to move it off his forehead, but one, the look was rather alluring, and two, it would've been too intimate of a gesture for someone I hardly knew.

Regardless, I was finding that Josh's bad boy persona was making me a little giddy. Liza had been right. Taking a few days off to forget my breakup and relax was starting to clear my mind and help erase the nerdy ex-boyfriend I'd been brooding about for weeks. Josh was anything but nerdy. His chest was broad, and his well-toned, tattooed biceps were calling to me. I wanted to run one of my long nails over them. It was odd that I was drawn to his tattoos. I'd never had a thing for tats. I could take them or leave them. Yet at the moment, I was really appreciating the reds and yellows of his tat that depicted an eagle clinging to an anchor, a pistol, and what looked like a pitchfork. Scripted underneath the elaborate tattoo were the words, "The Only Easy Day Was Yesterday." I knew that military Navy SEAL motto because of my brother.

Josh let go of my hand, causing me to jerk my head up to look at him. I was considered tall for a lady, but I wasn't as tall as him.

"Riley." His voice was husky, sending a gooey feeling straight south, not even stopping to tickle my stomach. "Liza called and told me you were on your way."

Any reaction I had to his voice went *poof.* "Really? She had her assistant call me." I shouldn't have been hurt that she hadn't bothered to call me, or maybe she had. I'd traveled through one or two cell dead zones on my way there. Yet I didn't have any messages on my phone.

He waved a hand toward the wicker-framed loveseat. I didn't hesitate as I commandeered an edge of the cushion, and set my purse on a matching wicker table that had a Reel Life pamphlet on it. At first I thought it was an advertisement on fishing. But a quick scan of the brochure explained how Reel Life was the new social media network for sharing photos and videos.

I was about to pick up the pamphlet when Charlie came up to me and sat on his hind legs. It was then I noticed the service dog insignia on his harness. I was aware of Josh's story. He'd been on a mission in Afghanistan when an explosion rocked the building he was in. According to Liza, he was lucky to be alive.

Josh wheeled my suitcase over and folded his body into the chair on my left. "Don't be too upset with her. She's been burning the midnight oil."

While I was a little put out by the sudden change in her plans, I knew stuff happened. I considered myself adaptable. I didn't get upset at much unless someone was hurting my family and friends, and I always looked on the brighter side of things.

My grandma was a firm believer in things happening for a reason. *"You may not know what that reason is, but nine times out of ten, good always comes in the end."*

Maybe the good from this would be that Liza would get a raise.

As for me, I was sitting with a gorgeous man who, upon closer inspection, was even more beautiful than I remembered seeing in photos. A hot guy, a cool dog, a beautiful place, and I didn't have anywhere to be the next morning. A girl couldn't ask for more than that. "I'm good. So is there a room available for me?" I scanned the lobby.

Voices filtered out of the restaurant. Pictures of celebrities like Clint Eastwood, Bill Murray, and others hung on the walls around me.

Josh cleared his throat. "I'm working on that."

My gaze rounded on him. "You mean you're booked." I shouldn't have assumed I had a room since I was supposed to be staying with Liza. I shouldn't have been surprised either. After all, the parking lot was full when I'd pulled in. "I can find another hotel."

He grinned as he finally moved that loose hair away from his forehead. "That's the thing. There's not a room within a thirty-mile radius."

Maybe I should plant myself on Liza's doorstep and wait for her to get off work. The problem was, I wasn't in the mood to get in the car. My body was shutting down fast.

Josh studied me as though he were trying to get in my head. His green eyes were roaming up, down, and all around.

I lowered my gaze to my red-painted toenails and tucked hair behind my ear. I normally didn't shy away from a man giving me the once-over. But with Josh, I found myself giddy and flirty like a teenage girl in high school.

As I stole a look at the man who was suddenly making my insides pitch, rattle, and roll in a good way, I remembered what Liza had told me about Josh's hearing. I should have remembered sooner, but I chalked up my forgetfulness to exhaustion and the handsome man in front of me.

"You can hear me?" I asked.

He chuckled, a sound that gave me goose bumps. Or maybe I was just chilled with the cross breeze blowing in from the open doors that spanned the length of the restaurant.

"I had some hearing return to my right ear, but it's not that good. I can hear if the sounds are loud enough, and when it comes to voices, the person has to be close to me. Or if you're my father, then shouting works too." One side of his mouth turned upward. "Your voice"—he licked his lips—"is melodic."

Heat pinched my cheeks. No one had ever told me that my voice sounded melodic. I'd had guys tell me I had nice breasts, curves, and legs, but never voice. I was tempted to ask him if that was his pickup line for all women, but he sounded genuine. I wasn't a smarty-pants either, although I could be with Liza and my brother and those I knew well.

"No hearing aid?"

"Hearing aids don't work on me. Anyway, I'll check to see if we have any cancellations."

Quick on my feet, I said, "I'll call Liza and head to her apartment in the city."

He dragged a hand over his rugged jaw that needed a shave. "Absolutely not. It's getting late, and you're here now. Let me see what I can do. In the meantime, why don't you grab a bite in the restaurant and relax."

I was famished, and I could use something cold to drink.

He and Charlie escorted me into the restaurant. It was then I noticed a slight limp in his gait.

Nevertheless, the short distance was painful on my feet. I was wearing mid-size high-heeled sandals, compliments of Liza. Since she worked for a swanky fashion company, she sometimes shipped me new product samples. The designer mules were stylish but not meant for a fourteen-hour day.

I groaned as Josh pulled out a chair for me.

Again, he let out a low chuckle, or maybe he groaned with me.

"Sorry, my feet hurt," I said.

"Charlie, stay," Josh commanded.

The golden retriever obeyed and lay down near me.

As Josh left, a waiter took my order of lemonade and a nacho appetizer. Then I called Ross and filled him in on where I was. After I hung up with him, I called Liza.

She answered on the first ring. "Sorry, bestie."

I could hear the anguish in her voice, so I couldn't get mad at her. Besides, the ocean view I had at the moment with the full moon shining over the water was far better than staying in the city with horns blowing and the din of traffic outside a window. If Josh couldn't find me a room, I was tempted to sleep in one of the rocking chairs on the veranda that Liza had bragged about.

The waiter, an average-size man, set down my lemonade.

I took a gulp. "When are you getting here?"

"Not until tomorrow," she said. "I have to finish something for a client. I should be out of work by noon."

I ran a finger along the glass that was sweating a little. "Why did you send me here and not your apartment? Are you dating someone that I don't know about?"

Silence reigned over the line before she sighed. "Josh will take care of you. Relax. I'm sure you're tired. I'll fill you in soon."

I took her answer as a yes. I couldn't help but wonder why she hadn't told me about him.

She's working. She doesn't have time right now.

That was the reason. We would have plenty of time to catch up starting the next day.

"You didn't tell me your cousin is drop-dead hot. I mean, I saw pictures, but wow!"

She giggled. "He needs a good woman like you. And you could

use a good man who will treat you like royalty and not trash like your ex." Anger filtered through her tone.

"Is Josh the reason you sent me here? Are you playing matchmaker?"

"I got to run. I should be at the inn by one tomorrow." Then she was gone.

A shiver zinged down my spine but quickly vanished when Josh returned.

His five o'clock shadow was getting darker. "Are you cold? I can get you a sweatshirt from the souvenir shop in the lobby."

My chill had nothing to do with being cold but rather with how Liza wasn't telling me something. And I had no idea what that something was.

"I'm good." I didn't want to mention anything to Josh. He might think I was a crazy woman. "So did you find a room?" *Please say yes.* I wanted to curl and sleep for twelve hours.

He frowned as Charlie perked up. "The only thing I can offer you is my place."

I choked. "Come again." I was all for having a good time with a man who was giving me goose bumps and making the butterflies inside my stomach flutter, but I didn't jump to second base on a whim. Sure, I was twenty-six years old and wasn't living in the Stone Age, but I had scruples. One of my absolute rules was that I had to know more about the guy than his name.

Granted, I knew more about Josh than the average man trying to pick me up in a bar, but I needed a little more meat to his story despite his gentlemanly qualities. Nevertheless, I was still giddy at the idea of sleeping at his place.

4

JOSH

Riley's scent of cherry blossoms was driving me mad as I lay in bed, staring at the ceiling. I swore her sweet smell was stuck to my nostrils, and I'd only escorted her from the inn to my dad's house a block north.

She'd been reluctant to take me up on my offer, but I couldn't have her driving into the city late at night. Like any big city, San Fran was easy to get lost in. I actually took comfort in knowing she was apprehensive. That showed me she didn't trust so easily, and that alone would keep her out of danger. I didn't know why I was even thinking about danger when it came to Riley. I had this over-whelming urge to protect her, and hell if I knew where that feeling was coming from.

I closed my eyes, willing sleep to come like I had every other night since I'd returned home from Afghanistan. I was mainly afraid to sleep for fear I would relive that explosion over and over again. Anytime I did, I always woke up in a cold sweat with pain gripping my leg.

Still, I had to get some shuteye, or else I would be useless at work the next day and at taking care of my dad. But he did have in-home health care four days a week, and tomorrow was one of those days, so I wouldn't have to tend to his every need.

Charlie curled up closer to me. I wrapped my arm around him and closed my eyes, my body finally giving in to sleep.

The apartment building was deathly quiet. The only sound was the creak of the stairs that I climbed with Wiggs, a brother at arms and a friend, behind me. We both had our guns at the ready, checking each apartment as we crept down the hall of the third floor, along the wall.

I was approaching an open door when a little boy ran out. I sucked in air, my arms tense, and my gun primed to fire.

His big brown eyes went wide.

I waved him off. "A boy is heading down," I said into my comm unit.

"Copy that," my lieutenant said.

I held up my fist, a signal to wait while I quickly poked my head into the open apartment door, once then twice. I pointed one finger forward, indicating that I was going in. Wiggs was on my heels.

The dingy place stunk of sweat and blood.

The word "clear" blared through my earpiece as others on my team checked the floors below.

I slowly looked around, turning my head with my gun out in front of me. I caught a glimpse of someone darting through the archway that led into the kitchen. I held up my fist again, but Wiggs bumped into me.

I pointed to the bedroom door, indicating that he should check the bedroom.

I proceed toward the kitchen. A floorboard groaned.

"Bandon," my lieutenant called in my earpiece. "Report."

I hated to utter a word, but at that point, the enemy knew I was inside.

"We've got movement in here."

"Is it our package?" Lieutenant asked.

Before I could respond, the man appeared, blocking my way into the kitchen. He was wrapped in explosives.

I froze. "Wiggs," I said as calmly as I could. "Get the hell out of here."

"Bandon." My lieutenant's voice was in my ear. "Report."

All I could think about was that I would never see my family again.

It was too late to run, too late to jump out the window, too late to say good-bye, and too late to plead with the young man to not press the trigger. I'd learned rather quickly that bargaining for a life with anyone in this country was useless.

So I gave in to whatever was about to happen because even if I got five feet away, I was a dead man.

"Lieutenant," I said as calmly as I could. "Please make sure my folks know that I love them."

He started shouting, saying something I couldn't make out because I was praying and shaking my head at the young man. Again, I knew no matter what I said, he wouldn't back down. But with a minute before my life was over, I had to give it the old college try.

"Please, don't do this."

His dark gaze studied me as though I were the weirdest person he'd ever seen. Then he blessed himself and pressed the detonator he was holding.

The world rained down around me.

Dog breath jolted me as I opened my eyes to find Charlie licking my face.

"I'm okay," I said to Charlie.

He jumped off the bed and ran through the Jack-and-Jill bathroom and into Dad's bedroom.

Worry flowed through me at breakneck speeds as I rushed behind Charlie. When I laid eyes on the scene before me, I froze. Actually, I winced when I should've been smiling at how Riley and Dad were chumming it up. The thing was, I was in my boxers.

Oh well. Boxers were like shorts anyway. At least my other body parts were cooperating properly. Still, I took in a big breath to get my heart to calm down. Between reliving my accident and thinking something had happened to Dad, I needed a minute.

I ducked out quicker than the speed of light so I could at least throw water on my face.

"Son," Dad called extremely loudly, which was normal since my hearing loss. "Don't be rude. We have a guest."

A beautiful guest, no less. "I'll be right there."

If Riley whispered or said something, I couldn't hear.

I would have given anything to hear faint noises, faraway voices, or even the howling of the wind. But there was no sense in brooding over something I couldn't change.

"Embrace life as it is today," my lieutenant had said when he visited me in the hospital. "You're lucky you're alive."

His last sentence was so true. I should've come home in a body bag, but I'd had an angel on my shoulder that dreadful day—a day I would relive over and over again.

I wiped my face as I glanced in the mirror. My green eyes were tired, with dark shadows ringing them. I needed a haircut badly, as my sideburns were growing out. I dampened my hands, tamed my hair, and threw on a pair of shorts before I waltzed back into Dad's room.

With my eyes a little more focused, I settled my gaze on Riley.

Her face lit up, and she gave me the most mind-blowing smile. My heart skipped a beat. It was the same feeling I'd had when Marybeth, my first love in high school, had glided into science class like a goddess. Her black hair had hung wild around her shoulders as her stark-blue eyes stood out against her snow-white skin.

Maybe that was why I was sweet on Riley, although her eyes were gray. Still, I loved how her hair was tied up in a bun with strands hanging here and there, giving her a messy look.

She rose, her baggy T-shirt with the words "Boston Strong" splayed on the front hung over her tight yoga pants. "I'm sorry. I didn't mean to wake you." She directed her statement at me. "I couldn't sleep anymore. The time change has my body clock all messed up. So I got up to get something to drink, and I heard your dad talking to Charlie."

Charlie wagged his tail.

My dad gave me the biggest grin as he drilled his gaze into me, trying to tell me something.

Whatever it was would have to wait. Awkwardness washed over me, and I had to do something other than stare at Riley. If I continued to, then all bets were off on how my body would react. "I'll make coffee."

She rose so eloquently, as if she were the Queen of England. "I'll do it. I think your dad needs to use the bathroom."

I cocked an eyebrow at Dad.

He nodded. "I do."

After all the essential bodily functions were taken care of and Dad was back in bed, he said, "That's a woman for you."

I fluffed his pillow. "No matchmaking. You know what happened when you tried to set me up with your buddy's daughter."

That had been the worst blind date ever—uncomfortable, tense, and neither of us had been into each other. It wasn't that she wasn't pretty, but she hadn't made my heart sing like Riley had when she'd walked into the inn. In fact, Riley was still making my pulse soar to new proportions.

"She's here for a few days. Get to know her and see what happens."

Charlie barked as if in agreement.

I eyed my lovable dog. I swore he understood what Dad was saying.

I kissed Dad on the forehead. "Get some sleep."

I left Charlie with Dad and went into the kitchen.

Riley seemed to be at home, getting the coffee cups out of the cabinet and checking the fridge for milk.

I slid into a chair at the round wooden table in the middle of the kitchen. Dad's house wasn't fancy with stainless-steel appliances or marble counters. We liked the older look of the black-and-white-checkered floor and old-style fridge from the 1950s. The only modern item in the kitchen was the coffeepot.

Riley filled two cups then brought them over to the table.

I watched in quiet fascination as she also gathered up the milk, sugar, and spoons before she sat down. I sifted through all my memories of women I'd dated, and I could count them on one hand. Besides Marybeth, there was a woman named Eve who'd only lasted a week before I shipped out for SEAL training. I wasn't a hermit, but I hadn't wanted to bring anyone into my life while I was on mission after mission. I'd seen one too many of my military brothers go home in body bags. It was bad enough that my mom had worried about me.

"I hope you don't mind that I made myself at home." Riley's tone was quiet, and so was the house, which gave me ample hearing. It helped that she was close to me too.

"For a woman who was apprehensive about staying here, I got to say, you sure settled in quickly. Not that I'm complaining."

She giggled, a sound that did things to me I was desperate to pursue. "Honestly, I didn't want to impose. My brother, Ross, might be mad that I did take you up on your offer." She dumped two big spoonfuls of sugar into her coffee, along with a ton of milk. "Actually, he wouldn't. He knows you're ex-military and a SEAL, so he would be in awe."

It was my turn to laugh.

"Ross wanted to be a SEAL."

I wanted to say there was nothing special about the job, but I would be lying. I loved being on missions—the adrenaline rushes, the camaraderie.

Charlie came in and sat next to me.

Riley took a sip of her coffee. "Thank you for letting me stay here. As soon as the sun comes up, I'm going to go into San Fran and meet Liza at her office."

I studied her lips. They were calling my name.

She waved her fingers in front of me. "Did you hear me? Or is my tone too low?"

She was sitting on my good side. "I did hear you. But just so you know, as long as you're close to me and on my right, I can hear you." *Or you can whisper in my right ear or, better yet, nibble on it.*

"Your dad shouted earlier, so I wasn't sure."

I gulped down a good amount of coffee. "It depends on the background noises. Liza told me she was coming here tomorrow. Did you talk to her? Did plans change?" I didn't want Riley to leave. In fact, I was tempted to steal her away from Liza while she was in town.

She shook her head. "We chatted while you were checking on rooms. She told me the same, but I was thinking I would surprise her."

Liza had said to take care of Riley, which gave me an idea. "Why don't I drive you in? The city can be quite intimidating with rush hour, especially on a Friday."

She studied me. "You know I live in Boston, where traffic stinks too."

"Yeah, but Liza would have my hide if anything happened to you. Besides, you're a guest in our neck of the woods."

The inn would be fine with Drake, and I had increased the shifts for Friday and Saturday. I also wanted to check on Liza. She'd seemed off when I'd spoken to her on the phone.

"If it's not too much trouble," Riley said with a hitch in her voice.

"Then it's a date." Maybe I could get to know Riley more, like Dad had suggested.

She blushed at my statement.

I took that as a good sign.

5

———————

RILEY

The city bustled with business people scurrying up and down sidewalks, horns blowing, and delivery trucks doubled parked. The atmosphere reminded me of home, which helped me lose some of the tension that had held me hostage since I'd arrived in Northern California.

Josh, Charlie, and I rode the elevator up to Stitches, Inc. on the fifteenth floor.

Josh held on to Charlie's leash as I clutched my purse. The car ride over had been mainly Josh talking about all the landmarks to visit in and around Northern California, in particular Lake Tahoe.

"It's too bad that you're not staying longer than four days," he'd said. "You would love Lake Tahoe. Liza's parents and mine used to vacation there, mostly in the winter during ski season."

I wasn't a skier. I couldn't even imagine me with skis on, even though I didn't live far from several well-known ski resorts in New England. Oceans were my love, not lakes. Summer was my season, not winter. I hated the bitter cold, the snow, and long nights during the winter months.

I wouldn't mind visiting Tahoe, and I got the feeling that Josh wanted to show me his childhood hangout.

The elevator dinged, and the doors opened to a shiny floor. An elaborate sign that read "Stitches, Inc." with a pair of scissors was etched into the glass wall behind the reception desk straight ahead.

Josh held one side of the elevator, allowing me to walk out first. It had been a while since I'd been around a man who opened doors for me.

A lovely lady of about fifty, with glasses perched on her nose, talked into a headset. When she noticed us, she held up her finger.

I took inventory of my immediate surroundings. Two hallways traveled down both sides of reception with doors spaced every few feet or so apart. I imagined we were on the executive floor and the rest of the employees were somewhere below us. Liza had talked about the dressing room as well as the drawing room where she spent most of her time.

"Are you sure Liza's office is on this floor?" I whispered in Josh's right ear. The place seemed dead.

His shoulder quivered. "I've only been here a couple of times."

"Then where is everyone?"

My question went unanswered as the receptionist asked, "How can I help you?" The gray streaks painted through her black hair glistened in the muted light.

"We're here to see Liza Bandon," I said.

"May I say who's calling?" the receptionist asked. "And do you have an appointment?"

Josh leaned a muscled arm on the glass counter, which acted as a barrier between us and the receptionist. "Josh Bandon and Riley Lewis, and no appointment."

The receptionist rose and eyed Charlie, then smiled. "I just love golden retrievers."

Charlie sat on his haunches, prim and proper and well obeyed, wagging his tail.

The receptionist waved her pink-painted fingernails to a small alcove near the elevators. "I'll see if Liza is available. Please have a seat over there."

Josh rested a hand on my lower back, and a jolt of electricity, delicious and out of the blue, sent tendrils of heat throughout my entire body. If his touch started a fire, his musky cologne was making me dizzy in a good way.

Four leather armchairs formed a circle in the alcove that was referred to as the waiting area. Josh waited for me to be seated before he commandeered the chair next to me.

Charlie nestled in between us as Josh fixed the purple bandanna around Charlie's neck.

We didn't have a chance to speak before a thin-as-a-rail blonde sashayed in, dressed as if she'd just stepped off the runway at a fashion show. Her pencil skirt, button-up white blouse, and silk red scarf complimented each other while accentuating her small curves. Her outfit screamed money and lots of it. I guessed the company paid their employees well.

She eyed Josh with big blue eyes that were framed with thick-mascaraed lashes. "Josh, so good to see you."

Josh stood and pecked her cheek. "Taylor." He glanced past her. "Where's my cousin?"

Taylor's red lips turned down. "I'm sorry to say she isn't here." Her gaze finally acknowledged me. "You must be Riley."

I rose, holding out my hand. "Nice to meet you."

She grasped my hand with both of her cold ones. "Liza has told me so much about you."

I couldn't say the same for her. Liza had never mentioned anything about her assistant.

"I hear you're a wedding planner," Taylor said. "I would love to pick your brain sometime. I just got engaged." She flashed a nice-sized round diamond at us.

I didn't want to be rude and ignore her interest in wedding planning, but we weren't there to talk shop. "Liza told me last night she would be working this morning."

"She was due in over an hour ago," Taylor said. "But I can't seem to get her on the phone." She tossed a look over her shoulder one way then the other. "I shouldn't be telling you this." Her voice was barely audible.

Josh inched closer to her with his right ear facing her.

"There were two men here yesterday, dressed in suits, looking for Liza." Taylor rubbed her lips together. "When I asked them who they were with, one of them said, 'We're friends of Liza's from Boston. We can't say much more than that."

My muscles tightened as nausea settled in my stomach. All I could think about was that the men were from Liza's old place of employment.

Before I'd left Boston, the news had been reporting that Stefano Moretti, Liza's former employer, had been arrested on tax evasion and money laundering. My mind was going down a lane that was making my pulse climb.

The FBI had questioned Liza after the raid on her former employer, Moretti Retailers, but she'd claimed she had never witnessed anything illegal while employed there.

Maybe the mafia family was trying to shut up all past and present employees so they wouldn't testify against their patriarch. I admit I'd watched a mafia movie a time or two, but it wasn't unheard of for someone like the mafia to shut up anyone who threatened their livelihood.

Taylor touched my arm. "Riley, you look pale. Do you know the men I speak of?"

"No." I didn't sound at all convincing.

Josh raised an eyebrow, those green eyes appraising.

I kept my thoughts to myself. For one, I didn't want to scare Taylor, who already had fear in her blue eyes; and two, I didn't want to come off as a crazy woman.

Josh whipped out his phone, tapped on the screen, and raised it to his ear. I imagined he was calling Liza.

I edged back from Taylor to get my mind clear and gulp down some air. "You told me on the phone that Liza was stuck in a meeting with a client yesterday. Is that true? Or was she in a meeting with these two men?"

"She's not answering her phone," Josh added. His tone was laced with concern. "What did they look like?"

She considered me first. "I told you the truth. And she never spoke to the men I mentioned. When I told them she wasn't available, they hesitated, exchanged some kind of look, and then left."

She turned to Josh, clasping her hands in front of her. "Both were tall. One was bald with a goatee. The other had thick black hair—handsome if you ask me. That's all I can tell you."

"Did they leave a card?" The mafia didn't leave calling cards. Their idea of a calling card was a dead person. But I asked just the same. Maybe they weren't who I was thinking of.

Taylor shook her head, and a stray blond hair came loose from behind her ear. "Nope."

The whoosh of the elevator doors sounded. An older gentleman donning a pinstriped suit waltzed in, carrying a briefcase.

"Look, I've got to run. As soon as she comes in or I hear from her, I'll call you," she said more to Josh than me. Then she darted off behind the man in the suit as though she were in trouble.

Josh threaded rugged fingers through his tresses. "Something is wrong. I can feel it."

I agreed. If Liza had to work, then she would be there. She was never late, but if she were, she would've called her assistant at least.

I gnawed on a nail, a habit of mine when I was nervous or thinking. "I say we check her apartment. Maybe she overslept."

Josh closed the short distance between us and gently grasped my wrist. "No need to worry."

I raked my gaze over him, angling my head. His tone earlier had hinted he was concerned, but he appeared calm, cool, and collected. I shouldn't have been surprised. After all, he'd been on deadly missions, and I suspected he'd been trained not to panic.

He guided my hand down then laced his fingers in mine. "I do have a key to Liza's apartment. When she travels, I'm her cat whisperer."

I giggled. He was handsome, a pure gentleman, compassionate, and he was slowly becoming a woman whisperer with the way he began tracing lazy circles on my palm with the tip of his finger.

Charlie wormed in between us, almost as if he wanted to hold my hand. Josh took his leash with his free hand, causing Charlie to walk on Josh's left.

The entire trek to my rental car, Josh kept his hand in mine. I swore if he let go, I might whimper. The last time I'd held anyone's hand was when I was with the guy before my ex. My ex wasn't a hand-holder. I found the act intimate, warm, and tingly.

Once we were in the car and the engine was running, Josh said, "Liza's fine."

"Are you trying to convince me or yourself?" I asked.

He engaged the gearshift. "Let's not think the worst. Sometimes Liza hangs out at a coffee shop near her place before she goes into work. She told me that she likes to catch up on emails before she hits the office."

I would've believed that if Taylor had heard from her.

6

———————

JOSH

I knocked on Liza's apartment door while Riley paced. She'd chewed her nails on the ride over. I was calm on the outside, but my antenna was up, and my gut was screaming that something was definitely wrong. I didn't want to show Riley I was just as freaked out as she was. I'd always been taught to stay calm in tense situations and not to draw conclusions before I had all the facts.

Charlie pawed me then raced over to the top of the stairs and ran back. Riley stopped in her tracks midway between the stairs and me. Then she hurried to see what Charlie was trying to alert me to.

I didn't have to look to know that someone was probably climbing the stairs. Liza's apartment building was only three floors with four apartments on each floor. So it was either Liza or someone who lived on her floor.

I knocked again as I kept my gaze trained on Riley and the stairs. Riley's shoulders were hunched up to her ears until the person came into view, then she chomped on a nail again.

A balding man, who looked to be in good shape, emerged. He was carrying a paper bag with a loaf of bread sticking out of the top. When he saw us, his gaze swung from Riley to me, then settled on Charlie, who was now next to me.

I grabbed Charlie's leash just in case the man was afraid of dogs. Charlie wouldn't hurt a fly unless someone was attacking me, and the old man didn't come across as someone who would hurt anyone.

I'd only been to Liza's apartment a handful of times, and I'd never paid attention or talked to any of her neighbors.

"If you're looking for Liza," the man said, "she left late last night."

All I could think was that she'd headed to the inn and her car broke down. Otherwise, my cousin wouldn't have left to go anywhere in the middle of the night.

Riley clutched her chest as if she were having a heart attack.

The old man stuck his key into the lock on the door next to Liza's. "Let me put my groceries down."

Riley rushed to my right side. "Late last night. What is going on? She wouldn't take off like that."

I wrapped my arm around her and drew her to me. "Breathe." I should have taken my own advice, but it was hard when Riley was pressed up against me. Now I was the one who needed oxygen.

"What if she decided to surprise me?" Riley pushed her body into mine as if she wanted to bury herself inside me.

My mind started down a path that wasn't appropriate at the moment.

"She could've gotten into an accident," Riley continued. "We should call the police."

We should, but we didn't know much yet, and there was a twenty-four hour window before the cops would do anything.

My gut twisted.

The old man returned, holding out his hand. "I'm Grayson. I just moved in not too long ago. How do you know Liza?"

I extended my hand. "I'm Josh Bandon, Liza's cousin. This is her friend, Riley."

After the intros, Grayson said, "She had a visitor last night about midnight. I couldn't sleep, so I sat out on my deck off my bedroom. I couldn't hear much. But I did hear her arguing with someone—a female if I'm not mistaken."

Riley and I exchanged a confused look.

The old man petted Charlie. "The argument didn't last long. I got the impression they knew each other."

"Did you happen to see the woman or anyone?" Riley asked.

"I'm sorry. I didn't."

I had no idea what our next move would be. I didn't know any of Liza's friends except Riley. The only person I could think of was Taylor. She was close to Liza since she was her assistant.

"Thank you, Grayson." I held up my key to Liza's apartment. "Riley and I are going to look around inside. If Liza does show up or you hear any activity inside later on, could you give me a call? I pulled out one of my business cards to the Redwood Cove Inn that I carried in my wallet.

Grayson read it. "I will. I do hope she's okay. She's a lovely person."

Once Grayson returned to his place, Riley and I went into Liza's. I blinked several times to make sure I wasn't seeing things.

Riley sucked in a sharp breath.

Charlie took off, searching the bedroom and bathroom for Liza's cat, something he always did when I came to feed Salem.

The cat screeched before she ran out of the bedroom with Charlie chasing her.

Normally, I would tell Charlie to leave Salem alone, but I was too dumbfounded at how trashed the living room and kitchen were. Furniture was turned upside down and kitchen drawers were left open, along with the cabinet doors.

Riley scraped a hand over her forehead. "I don't understand."

I didn't either. Then I remembered something. "Back at Liza's office when Taylor asked if you knew the men that paid Liza a visit yesterday, you said you didn't. But I agreed with Taylor that you turned white. What didn't you tell us?" I'd meant to probe more when we were in the car, but I'd been deep in thought, praying nothing had happened to my cousin.

Riley stepped over a lamp then settled at the window that over-looked the bay.

Liza lived in a swanky neighborhood in San Fran where views

of the Golden Gate Bridge poked out above the marine layer in the distance.

She hugged herself. "Did Liza fill you in on her former employer in Boston?"

I sidled up to her. "Yes. She worked for Stefano Moretti." When Liza had filled me in on what went down, I'd done some digging on the Internet. The family had been in the news quite frequently because of their ties to the cartel and other illegal business dealings. "The FBI raided the joint but didn't find anything to hold her boss on." I couldn't say I was surprised about her employer. My time as a SEAL had taught me that corruption was everywhere. But I'd been shocked that Liza had worked for the man. She hadn't known the company was owned by Moretti. Apparently, the company had been set up in his wife's maiden name.

Riley let out a nervous laugh. "Before I left to come out here, the news was reporting that Stefano Moretti was arrested for tax evasion and money laundering."

"And you think that has something to do with Liza?"

She shrugged.

Cars passed by below, and white caps crested on the surface of the bay beyond the traffic.

"Let's say for the sake of argument that you're right," I said, hoping beyond hope that Liza wasn't entwined in any mafia business. "Why would the Boston mafia track down Liza? She left them, and from what I understand from Liza, she had no blowback or interaction with the Moretti family after she quit."

Riley puffed out her rosy cheeks, her straight black hair hanging freely. I liked her hair down, but I preferred the updo style, which showed her long, smooth neck. "Call it a hunch. Maybe Moretti wants to be sure no employee, past or present, testifies against him. The FBI put Liza through the ringer."

"But she told the Feds she hadn't seen or had knowledge of any illegal activity."

"Unless she did and didn't tell us," Riley said.

At that thought, my stomach churned like a bad day at sea, and I'd had a few of those during my time as a SEAL.

I scanned the room. Charlie was lying down next to Salem, or rather Salem was nestled into Charlie's belly.

I rubbed two fingers across my chin. "Given how this place has been ransacked, I'm guessing someone thinks Liza has something of value." Whether any of this was related to the mafia in Boston or not, I wasn't sure.

Tears clouded Riley's gray eyes.

I gently grabbed her shoulders and bent my head slightly. "Hey." I tipped up her chin with the pad of my finger. "We'll find her."

Riley sniffled then threw her arms around me. "I'm scared."

Closing my eyes, I rubbed her back. It had been too long since I'd had a woman in my arms, and it felt amazing. I eased back, holding her face in between my palms. Her skin was silky and smooth.

She studied me, her gaze roaming back and forth and up and down.

The only body part I had in my scope was her lips—plump, pink, and so very kissable. The mess around us disappeared, and the only thing I could focus on was to kiss her or not to kiss her. *If I do, will she slap me? Should I ask permission first? A gentleman always asks first.* Dad had always counseled me on women. "Son, when it comes to women, treat them with respect. And never assume she wants the same thing you do."

But I didn't have to think at all when Riley pressed her lips to mine so softly and tentatively, I swore I was imagining it. Magic came to mind. In that moment, I felt as if I were in a fairy tale and she'd cast a spell on me, because I couldn't move. All I could think about was her and me and the magic we could make.

She jumped away. "I'm so sorry. I didn't mean to kiss you. I'm so emotional right now."

I touched my lips, which were on fire along with my body.

She wasn't getting away that easily. I tugged her to me. "You don't need to be sorry." I combed my fingers through one side of her hair until my hand rested on her neck.

Her gray eyes met my green ones as she sucked in her bottom lip, an act that was so darn sexy it made every cell in me come alive.

Walk away, man. You're supposed to be taking care of her on Liza's request, not making out with her. Then I stiffened. Riley had a boyfriend.

She frowned. "What's wrong?"

"It's none of my business. I thought you had a boyfriend back home." *Please say no.*

"Not anymore."

All my muscles loosened because luck was on my side. Then my phone vibrated in my jeans pocket. I dug it out. "Drake, is everything okay?"

"Um. Kind of." His tone said it wasn't. "Your dad's caretaker had to leave because of an emergency, so he's at the inn with me. Are you on your way back?"

There wasn't much we could do at Liza's other than call the cops about the break-in, although I wasn't sure it was a break-in. The mess could've happened the night before when Liza was arguing with that woman Grayson had mentioned.

"I'm leaving now." I ended the call.

My dad would be fine at the inn. On many days, he spent time in the office, doing accounting and helping out where he could since he could still use his hands. But the inn was probably busy, and Dad had a knack for getting in the way, especially when he started telling everyone what to do.

"Everything okay? Is it Liza? Is she at the inn?" Riley held her breath.

I wrapped my arms around her. "My dad's caregiver had to leave early."

Her hands ended up under my T-shirt on my lower back.

Goose bumps fired up my arms. If we didn't separate, I would probably go against my gentlemanly manners. "Let's head back. We'll regroup. I should take Salem with us." Reluctantly, I let go of Riley and made quick work of getting Salem's crate.

Riley gathered her hair and twisted it up on her head before securing it with a band she had around her wrist. "Should we call the police? This mess could be a result of a robbery." She was learning to raise her voice around me.

I'd been in Liza's place several times. I poked my head into

Liza's bedroom. Except for her nightstand drawer, everything else seemed to be in place, including the TV.

"I doubt anything was taken. Let's give it twenty-four hours." I couldn't recall if I'd mentioned lip reading to Riley. "By the way, I can read lips too." *And I'll be riveted to yours.*

Her mouth formed a perfect O.

I checked the door. "If it was a break-in, then it was an expert." The lock didn't show any signs that it had been tampered with.

Riley rolled back her shoulders. "I'm staying here and waiting."

She gave me the vibe that she was a strong woman, and that she could handle herself. Regardless, I wasn't leaving her alone. If in fact someone had broken in and hadn't found what they were looking for, then they might be watching the place.

"I'd rather you not," I said as I put Salem in her crate.

Charlie watched me intently.

"Then stay with me," Riley said.

My body was saying yes, but the logic in me was saying no. I had a lot of willpower, but I was afraid being alone with Riley would lead us to the bedroom, and while that was something I would like to happen, it was too soon. Not only that, but if I spent one night with Riley, I would be madly in love with her.

7

———

RILEY

I couldn't eat. I could barely keep still. The only saving grace I had going for me was a walk on the beach, alone, with the wind in my face, my toes in the sand, and the cold Pacific sliding over my toes every now and then.

Josh had convinced me to return with him to Redwood Cove. The only reason I did was because he promised we would do some detective work after he took care of his dad and made arrangements to have someone look after him.

I considered myself a strong woman and felt I could handle just about anything. I was finding I didn't have nerves of steel.

So many questions filtered through the haze that had settled in my brain. Who was the woman Liza was arguing with? Was it the same woman who had ransacked her apartment? Why would she leave in the middle of the night? Who were the men from Boston?

In all the phone conversations Liza and I had had, I couldn't recall one in which she'd sounded scared. She certainly hadn't mentioned Stefano Moretti or anyone who was giving her trouble.

I wondered if the client she'd met with the day before was the same one she'd been arguing with in her apartment, because she'd given me no indication that she would leave me hanging once I arrived, or that she might have to work while I was visiting. In fact, she'd been as overly excited as I was to spend time with each other.

The wind whipped around as a wave crashed along the shore. I jumped out of the way but not fast enough. Water splashed high, catching the edge of my capris.

On top of everything else, I had kissed Josh. I'd actually kissed the man, and boy, did I enjoy that. His lips were smooth, although I could feel him tense. I had no idea what had come over me. It had felt as though I'd had someone behind me, pushing me into him. I wasn't usually forward with men. Yet Josh was breaking that mold.

My phone rang as I was heading back to the inn. "Hey, Ross."

"Are you okay? You sound like something happened."

My brother knew me well.

"We can't find Liza. We think her apartment was broken into. I'm worried out of my mind."

"I'm getting on a plane," he said without hesitation.

I pushed my hair out of my face. "You can't just take off from your job." Ross worked for a private boarding school where the elite sent their kids to live and study for the school year. Ross was in charge of the boys' dorm, and it was time for kids to start returning for the fall semester.

"You let me worry about that."

I stopped on the deserted beach and dug my toes in the sand as I looked at the inn in the distance. "Josh is here with me. He'll protect me." I knew that was what my brother wanted to hear, and it was true. I trusted Josh implicitly.

"Where are you staying?" Ross asked.

I hadn't told him I was actually sleeping in one of the bedrooms in Josh's house, or rather Josh's father's house. Not that I was keeping it from him. When I'd spoken to Ross yesterday, I'd thought I would be staying at the inn or a hotel close by. But I didn't lie to my brother. He would know if I did anyway.

"The Redwood Cove Inn is booked, as are all the hotels around here, so Josh's dad had an extra room for me at his house not far from the inn."

"I don't like any of this." Ross sounded as nervous as my stomach was feeling.

"Me staying with Josh's father, or Liza?"

"You out there all by yourself with a stranger."

"Josh is the ex-Navy SEAL you're so enamored with. Don't worry."

Silence stretched over the line. I started for the inn again.

"You like him. Don't you?" Ross asked as I heard boys shouting in the background.

"Where did that come from?" He was spot on, but I didn't necessarily want him to know it.

"Sis, I heard it in your voice when you said he would protect you."

"Sue me, then," I teased. "He's a nice guy, but I only just met him."

So what? asked the little voice in the back of my head.

"The dorms are filling up, it sounds like."

My brother didn't need to hear how I was attracted to Josh, or that I'd already seen the man in his boxers, with sleepy eyes, bedhead, and a naked chest.

I blushed. I'd gotten all excited, and my mind had drifted to other things I wouldn't dare say out loud.

"Don't change the subject," Ross said. "Look, it's nice that you're taking time off, but be careful not to fall for someone when you know that long-distance relationships never work." My brother, ever the realist.

I laughed. "Says the relationship guru who can't seem to hold down a girlfriend."

"Call me tonight. I got to go." He didn't give me a chance to say another word.

That was probably a good thing. We would only get into an argument about relationships. He would tell me he needed to approve of the man I married. In turn, I would say the same thing about the woman he settled down with.

Josh was waiting for me with a grin the size of California when I climbed the porch steps to the back of the inn.

I lowered my gaze and tucked hair behind my ear.

"I love when you blush," he said. "It's so darn cute."

Hmm. Cute. When I thought of cute, I thought of Liza's cat, a pixie, or a puppy. I had a barb or two on my tongue but decided that a compliment was a compliment no matter the semantics. After all, cute by definition did mean attractive, gorgeous, and pretty.

Instead of shouting out any reply, I went up to him, lifted up on my tiptoes, and whispered in his right ear. "Thank you." His manly scent created waves of goose bumps up and down my arms.

He visibly quivered.

I edged back and found hunger—strong, raw, and powerful—living deep in his green eyes. He blinked once, shook his head, then sighed. Strands of his hair fell forward.

In that moment, images of us entwined in each other's arms played like a Nicholas Sparks movie in my mind.

He raked his gaze over me, slowly and tentatively. It felt as if he were dragging his fingertips over my skin ever so lightly.

Something was happening between us, and whether it was lust or a strong like for one another, I could see us walking down the aisle in a church with our friends and family around us.

"Stop analyzing your life and future," I shouted in my head. *"You just met him."*

That might have been true, but I felt as if I'd known Josh for a long time. Maybe because Liza had talked about him in many of the conversations we'd had.

But I was getting ahead of myself, and I shouldn't since I was only in California for a few days. Ross was right. Long-distance relationships didn't work. I'd seen it firsthand with my mom. After her bitter divorce, she'd met a guy who lived in St. Louis. They had dated for six months before they'd called it quits. She hadn't wanted to leave Boston, and he'd had kids in St. Louis. They'd parted ways on good terms, although she'd pined for him for months afterward.

I wasn't tied to Boston, but I couldn't imagine leaving my brother or my mom and not seeing them for months or only on holidays.

If you don't find Liza, then you might be here longer, which would be a good thing for you and Josh.

Excitement bubbled to the surface at the idea of Josh and me, but fear pushed it down. No matter how attracted Josh and I were to one another, we couldn't pursue a relationship of any kind until we found Liza.

"Are you ready to do some detective work?" I asked.

Voices trickled out of the restaurant.

One side of Josh's mouth turned upward. "Let's head into the city. We should talk to Taylor again and see if she's heard from Liza. Then we can swing by her apartment one more time."

I didn't care what we did as long as we were doing something to find Liza. "I know it hasn't been twenty-four hours, but in a matter of hours, it will be." My tone was higher than normal just in case he wasn't getting all that by reading my lips. "So let's try filing a missing person's report anyway. Oh, and if Grayson heard arguing, then maybe some of the other residents saw something or heard something. We should go door to door."

He lifted a muscled shoulder that was covered in a dark-blue T-shirt with the words "Honor, Courage, Bravery" and a Navy SEAL printed on the front. "Sounds good. Have you tried calling Liza again?"

I'd dialed Liza's number repeatedly on our way out of the city, and the line had gone to voice mail each time. Frustration was becoming madness the more time passed.

"I'll try calling her again in the car," I said. "Is your dad going to be okay?" I didn't want Josh leaving if his dad needed him. I knew ALS was a terrible disease. The dad of one of my clients had ALS, and she'd wanted to get married before her dad lost his ability to walk.

Josh held out his hand. "Yes."

When my palm met his, all tension, fear, despair, and panic faded, at least for the moment.

8

JOSH

I had to call the in-home health care company to see if I could hire another caretaker to help my dad. Guilt rode me hard at leaving my father with someone else, but I explained to him about Liza and that she could be in trouble. He didn't mind being left with a stranger. He would probably talk the guy's ear off anyway.

I also had Drake on standby in case the nurse who'd shown up an hour ago had to leave early for some reason.

Drake was as distraught as Riley and me were that Liza could be missing. I was holding out hope, even though I had an eerie feeling coursing through me. It was so unlike my cousin not to answer her phone or at least let someone know what was going on. She wouldn't have ditched Riley either. She had planned every activity for her and Riley, and she wouldn't have just fallen off the face of earth.

Regardless, my brain was having a hard time comprehending that someone would hurt my sweet cousin.

"I should call my brother," Dad had said. "He'll want to know about his daughter."

"Please don't until I can find out more," I'd said.

Liza's father didn't give her the time of day, but I agreed with my dad that his brother should know more about his daughter. I doubted he would rush to the Bay Area from Sacramento, but I could hear the argument now.

"You knew my daughter was missing and didn't bother to tell me?" my uncle would ask. Unless he was drunk, he would brush off his daughter like a piece of lint on a dark suit.

Riley waved a hand in my face. "Earth to Josh."

Rubbing a temple, I braked in traffic.

Riley reached over the console and squeezed my thigh.

Instantly, the blood rushed through me, almost kick-starting my heart. The woman was no doubt bringing out feelings in me that I hadn't experienced in years. While it felt good to have someone comforting me, I took a breath. Part of me wanted to capitalize on her actions and kiss her, as in really and truly kiss her. We'd been interrupted when I had attempted to earlier that day.

But I was driving, and we had more pressing matters in front of us too. I needed to take a step back and reel in my feelings. Otherwise, I would ask her to marry me before she even left the state.

So I covered my hand over hers and grinned. "It's great to have you here. I wish the situation was better, though."

She withdrew her hand and dragged her soft fingers down my rough jaw. I wasn't one to grow a beard quickly, but I had the beginnings of a five o'clock shadow.

"I try to look on the bright side of things. Maybe we were destined to be in this position." Her voice sounded as silky as her skin felt.

Charlie perked up in the back seat as though he were alerting me to her voice. But Riley was on my right, and we were confined in a small space. I had no problem with hearing. It felt as though I was in tune to her even if I couldn't hear her.

Riley abandoned me for Charlie. "We're almost there, boy."

He licked her hand. Suddenly, I wanted to be Charlie. I wanted Riley to run her hands through my hair like she was doing to Charlie. Then a laugh broke out in my head. I was jealous of my dog.

Traffic started moving a little faster.

"I'm praying Liza is cleaning up her apartment," I said more to myself and to break the spell Riley had me under. Despite that, I'd been praying all day that Liza would return my call since we'd left about a hundred messages. I wasn't exaggerating either. Among Drake, Riley, and me, we'd called her repeatedly.

Riley flopped back against the passenger seat of her rental car that had the lingering new-leather scent. A stray black hair came undone from the updo she was sporting. Her pink-colored blush makeup was swept across her cheeks perfectly, giving her a soft glow. She had the perfect profile—round chin, small nose, and high cheekbones.

Traffic still crawled as we approached the Golden Gate Bridge.

Riley tapped on her phone. "I'm calling Taylor." After a second, Riley said, "Taylor, please." Another beat of silence followed. "The line goes straight to her voice mail. I think Taylor isn't telling us something."

"What makes you think that?" I'd known Taylor since Liza hired her about six months ago. She seemed like a good person—honest, dedicated, and professional.

"During our conversation with her, I found it odd when she said, 'I shouldn't be telling you this.' Then she proceeded to tell us about the two men. Why would that be a secret? Did those men threaten Liza or Taylor or both of them? And she looked around as though someone was watching her. I think Liza was in a meeting with those men and not an important client like she had Taylor tell me. And remember, those men were from Boston. They have to be Moretti's men."

I leaned my elbow on the middle console. "So you think Liza lied to us? And if you're right about Moretti's men, then Taylor could be in danger too."

I didn't know a whole lot about the mafia world. What I did know was that eliminating a person was their way of dealing with anyone who threatened or compromised their organization.

"I think Liza didn't want to worry us," Riley said.

Or maybe she'd had a gun to her head when she'd called me. She hadn't sounded like herself.

By the time we arrived at Stitches Inc., it was almost the end of the workday. Then again, Liza had been known to work late.

A short woman with fiery-red hair pushed in her chair at the reception desk. "I'm sorry. We're closing."

She wasn't the same lady Riley and I had met earlier that day. This woman was much younger and seemed to have a chip on her shoulder.

I held on to Charlie's leash. "We're here to see Taylor or Liza." *Please let Liza be here.*

She hiked her bag on her shoulder, circled the desk, and ushered us toward the elevator. "Taylor left at lunch and hasn't returned. Liza hasn't been in all day." She stabbed the elevator button.

"You're not the same lady from earlier today." Riley sounded suspicious. "How many receptionists work here?"

"We have a few," the redhead said.

That was probably true. I'd seen a couple of different ladies at the desk when I'd visited Liza in the past.

The elevator doors opened.

Riley blocked the woman from getting in the elevator. "We need Taylor's home address."

I held in a grin at how Riley wasn't leaving the building without getting what she wanted. And I really enjoyed that her deep New England accent was coming out in full force.

The redhead studied Riley as if she had four heads. "Seriously. I can't give you that information."

The doors closed.

"Even if it's life or death?" I asked.

The petite lady nodded. "I could lose my job."

Riley pursed her lips, narrowing her eyes. "How would you feel if something happened to Taylor and we could've prevented it but in the end couldn't because you wouldn't help us?"

The two women were in somewhat of a standoff, giving each other the stink eye.

I was about to appeal to the receptionist when she slumped her shoulders and stomped back to her desk. "I need your names and addresses."

Riley and I swapped perplexed looks.

As if the lady knew what we were thinking, she said, "If I lose my job, I'm coming to find both of you."

The woman was hilarious. She was a tiny thing who couldn't hurt a fly. Despite that, I gave her the address to the Redwood Cove Inn. "That's where you can find us." She didn't need to know much more than that, or that Riley lived in Boston.

While the redhead was searching her computer, Riley leaned into my right ear. "Do you know where Liza's office is? Maybe we should snoop around."

Her breath on my ear was energizing, and that magic spell she'd had me under in Liza's apartment started to cloud my senses. The urge to pull her to me and feel her against me was overpowering. But this wasn't the time or place. Man, I was falling hard and fast. My mom had always believed in love at first sight. The minute she'd laid eyes on my dad, she'd known he was the one.

My hand snaked around Riley's waist to settle on her lower back. It was my turn to whisper in her ear. "Hold Charlie. I know where Liza's office is. Keep Red occupied." I wanted to stay in this position so I could nibble on her earlobe and explore more of her.

"Later," my brain shouted.

She dipped her head just as I was pulling away, and my lips brushed against her ear.

She spewed a noise or a moan.

Man, I was in trouble.

I shook off the lust-filled bubble she had me in and strutted up to Red. I glanced down both hallways, but all seemed quiet. I was beginning to wonder if anyone actually worked on that floor. Sure, I'd been in Liza's office a time or two, but even then, I hadn't seen many people on the floor.

"I need to use the restroom." I started heading down the hall where Liza's office was located, as was a men's room, if I remembered correctly. "I know where it is," I tossed over my shoulder.

"Make it quick," she said rather loudly.

Adrenaline spiked through me as though I were on a mission, and I couldn't help but grin. I missed everything about being a

SEAL—the camaraderie, the planning, the anticipation before we shipped out, and the mission itself.

I placed my hand on the men's room door then checked on Red, who was writing on a piece of paper. Riley was leaning up against the counter, and Charlie was staring at me.

I wanted to tell him I wasn't in any danger and didn't need his help, but when Riley began petting his head, he looked up at her.

I ducked into the bathroom and waited, counting to ten. Then I poked out my head in one quick motion, a habit I had when checking rooms in buildings while on a mission.

The reception desk was empty. As quietly as I could, I hurried down to Liza's office, which was two doors down. I gripped the handle then turned. Relief traveled through me that at least the door wasn't locked. Before I went in, I took a breath as memories of that fatal day in Afghanistan bombarded me.

You're in an office building of a fashion company, not in a place where bombs strapped to enemies are the norm.

Nevertheless, I glanced down the long hall one more time. The coast was still clear.

Once inside Liza's office, I blew out a breath, mainly because a bomb hadn't gone off. Then I crossed the carpeted floor, skirting around racks of clothes and a slanted table that had Liza's latest dress design drawn out on paper. One of the reasons Liza had moved to Boston was for fashion school.

I settled behind her desk, quickly sweeping my gaze over the contents. Sticky notes covered the perimeter of her computer screen.

Riley's flight info was on one. "Call Haley" was on another. "Get Taylor to run down to Berger's fabric shop." "Talk to Monroe." "Prep for fashion show."

Nothing stood out to me, and since her desk was one solid piece of glass, no drawers existed. I was about to peek into a filing cabinet that was located near the floor-to-ceiling window not far from me when Charlie's wet nose pushed on my hand. My heart skipped a beat as I zeroed in on Candace, who had a scowl the size of California.

She crossed thin arms over her chest. "What are you doing? I should call the cops!" she practically shouted.

Riley came to an abrupt halt behind the lady, mouthing, "I'm sorry."

Charlie wagged his tail at my side.

Stupid me for not bringing him with me, although by the time he would've alerted me to any noise, it would've been too late.

I held up my hands. "Look, I know you're only doing your job. But my cousin, Liza, is missing. And whether your job is on the line or not, I don't care. I need to find her."

"I've given Riley Taylor's address. I have your info. If I hear anything, I will call you." She waved her hand at the door. "Now you both need to leave."

I grabbed Charlie's leash.

Maybe we would have better luck with Taylor.

9

RILEY

"The redheaded receptionist, Candace, was rather sweet," I said to Josh as he opened the door of Taylor's apartment building. When Josh had gone to the bathroom, I'd apologized to Candace for being a witch and told her how worried I was about Liza. After that, she had lowered her guard until she'd caught Josh in Liza's office.

Josh stabbed the up button on the elevator. "So you two bonded."

The lobby area was rather dirty. Paint was chipping off the walls, and the elevator sounded as though it was on its last leg as it arrived.

The first thing that came to mind was that the company wasn't paying Taylor enough money. The way she dressed, though, led me to believe she was paid well.

I could continue the small talk about Candace and how she was engaged, but my mind was stuck on Taylor and the rundown building and neighborhood she lived in, which was a far cry from Liza's upscale place.

"Do you find it weird that Taylor lives in a dingy place that's seconds away from crumbling?" I was making it a habit to always be on Josh's right side so he could hear me.

The elevator moved slowly on its ascent.

"It's expensive to live in the city." He sounded detached.

"You know the sky is blue," I returned.

"Yeah" was all I got. No jerk of his head, smile, or anything to indicate he was aware of my sarcasm.

I dragged my nails down his back.

He flinched then fixated on my lips. "Do that again, and you might not get off this elevator."

Promises, promises. "Where are you? I just said the sky is blue. You've been quiet since we left Liza's office."

He chuckled. "Thinking. Has Liza ever mentioned a Haley or Monroe? I saw their names on sticky notes on her desk."

The doors opened on the fifth floor.

I knew a Haley. "Haley is a gal Liza used to work with at Moretti Retailers. I never heard the name Monroe."

Burn holes dotted the carpeted hallway, and the floor creaked as we approached apartment six.

Taylor's voice boomed behind the green door. I didn't know if Josh could hear her, but Charlie nudged his hand before sniffing the threshold.

"Is something going on inside?" he asked.

I sharpened my hearing.

"You weren't supposed to do that," Taylor said.

"It sounds like she's arguing with someone," I said.

Suddenly, Grayson's words hit me. Maybe Taylor was arguing with the same person Liza had been.

Josh pounded his fist instead of knocking.

Taylor's voice died.

A minute passed, and we heard nothing.

Josh banged again. "Taylor, open up. It's Josh."

After one click and a squeak, the door creaked open. Taylor had her cell phone to her ear. "I got to go." She lowered her phone. "How did you get my address?"

I scanned her apartment as best I could from the hallway. The place was empty from what I could see. "Candace, one of the receptionists at your office."

Josh pushed his way past Taylor. "Who were you arguing with? Liza?"

Taylor mashed her glossy lips into a thin line. "Hey, you can't just barge your way in."

Josh let go of Charlie, who took off into the bedroom.

Taylor ran after Charlie. "My cat is in there, and she doesn't like dogs."

Josh hurried to get Charlie. "Hey, boy."

I stepped in, taking inventory of the sparse apartment. The room had a fabric chair, a narrow end table, one stool at the bar that overlooked a kitchen, a stove, a fridge, and nothing else. The place was drab and felt cold and detached.

The cat screeched and came running out with Taylor trying to grab her furry tan-and-white animal.

Charlie trotted out with Josh holding his leash.

Once Taylor scooped up her cat, she cooed, "I'm sorry, Ivy."

"Sit," Josh said to Charlie, who obeyed his master.

"Why are you here?" Taylor asked as she put Ivy back into the bedroom and closed the door.

Josh walked around the kitchen, almost acting as if he thought Liza was hiding in a cabinet.

"We wanted to see if you've heard from Liza," I said, not moving from the door. "We were also worried. If I'm right about the men from Boston, you could be in trouble since you work for Liza."

Taylor sat on the arm of the dilapidated chair. "Thank you for your concern, but I'm fine. And I talked to Liza earlier today. She was on her way back to her apartment. Apparently, she had a client meeting in the city that I didn't know about."

My jaw came unhinged. "Why didn't you call us?" I was ready to scream. "We've been worried out of our minds."

She picked at a nail. "I've been busy. I still have a job to do."

Josh crossed his arms over his chest and gave her a death stare. Even angry, he was handsome.

My intuition was telling me something wasn't right with Taylor, but I couldn't pinpoint what. Still, a sense of relief washed over me, but it didn't stick. I wanted to believe her, but I knew Liza. She would've called me. She wouldn't have left me hanging, especially when we had plans and I'd traveled all this way.

I gripped the strap of my cross-body bag. "What time did you talk to her?"

"Around noon. Look, I have to meet my fiancé for dinner."

Maybe he was the person she'd been raising her voice to on the phone.

"You don't sound all that concerned about Liza," Josh said.

"I have my own problems going on. Besides, she sounded fine on the phone, although she was in a hurry. She said she was late in meeting you." She pointed at me.

Charlie guarded the bedroom door as though he wanted to protect Ivy.

"Obviously, she didn't meet me." The sarcasm tumbled out. My nerves were fried. My stomach was all in knots, and I had that bad feeling I'd gotten at the airport, multiplied a million times over.

I plucked my phone out of my purse and tapped on Liza's number for probably the thousandth time that day. The line immediately went to her voice mail.

Josh glanced at me. "No answer?"

I shook my head. "Taylor, when we spoke at the office this morning, you mentioned the two men from Boston. Why weren't you supposed to say anything about them?"

She was still fidgeting with a nail. "Liza didn't want anyone to know."

I rubbed my neck. The day was catching up with me, and tiredness was setting in. "So Liza knew the men?"

"She knew one of them," Taylor said, matter-of-factly. "She wouldn't tell me anything more than that.

"Did Liza speak with them?" Josh asked.

"No. As I said, they left without speaking with Liza."

Josh bit on his lip. "If they didn't speak with Liza, then how did she know one of them?"

Great question.

Taylor toyed with her one-carat diamond. "I described them to Liza."

I understood that rent could be high in the city, but everything about Taylor said she came from money or had money.

As far as I was concerned, Taylor was my number-one suspect. Regardless, we could probe her for hours. She wasn't going to tell us anything else. Besides, if Liza was at her apartment, we had a chance to catch her since she wasn't answering her phone.

Once we were outside, I asked, "Do you think she's telling us the truth about talking to Liza?"

"Not sure," Josh said. "Maybe Liza's into something we don't know about."

I prayed she wasn't doing work for the mafia.

10

———————

JOSH

When I pulled into a spot across from Liza's place, I noticed two men sitting in a black SUV. Riley had her hand on the door handle, eager to see if Taylor was telling the truth.

"Wait," I said.

She flashed her gray eyes my way. "What's wrong?"

"I think we have company in the black SUV two cars down and across the street."

Riley sat back, smoothing a hand over her hair. "The men from Boston?"

The car could have been government, mafia, or anyone. "Don't know. I can't make out who it is from here." The windows were slightly tinted. "Wait here with Charlie. I'll run in and see if Liza's home."

Riley grabbed my arm. "I think we should stick together." Her calm voice belied the fright in her eyes.

"Get behind the wheel. I want you to get out of here if anything happens." I prayed that nothing would, but the warning signs were going off in my head. The people in that car had to be watching for Liza.

Riley's pretty features turned dark. "I'm not leaving you here."

I placed my palm on her cheek. "Baby doll, I know how to handle myself."

She leaned into my hand. "You should at least take Charlie."

I should have, but Charlie would slow me down. "I won't be long." I rubbed my thumb over her smooth cheek.

Her eyelids became heavy. "What if you can't hear someone coming up behind you?"

I sat back. "Give me your phone." When she did, I punched in my number then called myself so I would have her number. "Text me if those guys follow me in." Then I darted out before I changed my mind and had her come with me, and before I kissed her.

I kept my head down, ignoring the men. I didn't want to call attention to myself, and I wanted to make it look as if I lived in the building. I fired a quick look over my shoulder at Riley before I entered. She'd gotten behind the wheel.

Good girl.

I gave a passing glance to the black SUV, but I still couldn't see the people inside clearly. My gut was telling me that Liza wasn't home. Or maybe she was, and those men were waiting for her to leave. Either way, I rushed up to the third floor, taking the steps two at a time. I didn't want to leave Riley alone for too long.

But she was right. I probably should've taken Charlie with me. At least he could've alerted me to noises or someone following me. Deep down, though, I didn't want to put him in harm's way. He wasn't an attack dog, although he was protective of me.

I made it to Liza's door when my phone vibrated in my jeans pocket. My pulse quickened. I had no way to protect myself other than my fists. I felt naked without all my tactical gear, something I'd thought I would never need again. But as the hours passed with no signs of my cousin, I had a feeling I would need some type of weapon to protect Riley and me.

With my lack of hearing, the only thing going for me was my sense of smell, and that only worked if the person had any kind of body odor or was wearing perfumes or colognes.

Liza's apartment was still a mess, and there were no signs of life.

I was glad I'd taken Salem home. She was currently lounging with my dad.

"Liza?" I called as I fished out my phone.

A text from Drake said, *Did you find Liza?*

I didn't have time to answer him. I checked the bedroom and bathroom, inhaled a few times to see if there were any fresh smells of anyone, including my cousin, who always wore a flowery perfume.

I got nothing. Walking out of the bedroom, I froze.

Two police officers had guns drawn on me.

Instinctively, I raised my hands.

The cop with the larger build didn't move while his partner cuffed me.

"I can explain," I said. There was no use fighting them off. I would only end up in jail.

Once I wasn't a threat, both cops did a quick sweep of the place. The thinner cop returned to me, while his partner started talking into his radio.

I couldn't hear what he was saying, and I didn't have to. He was probably reporting what they'd found so far.

The one in front of me moved his lips, but he wasn't talking loud or close enough for me to hear.

So I angled my head.

In a flash, his hand was on his gun at his side.

"I can't hear all that well. You need to talk into my right ear. Or speak up."

He visibly relaxed. "Name," he practically shouted.

"My girlfriend is outside." The word girlfriend came out easily, as if Riley and I had been dating forever. The thought of her being my girl appealed to me in so many ways. *She lives in Boston. Long-distance relationships don't work.* "Can I make sure she's all right? Then I'll answer all your questions."

"That's not how this works," he said.

The name on his uniform read Tanner. "Officer Tanner," I said politely. "You can arrest me, but please, I need to make sure she's okay. She's in a blue Honda with my service dog."

One eyebrow rose. "Hodge," Tanner said to his partner. "Can you check a blue Honda outside?"

Hodge nodded, revealing a double chin as he stalked out.

I slumped my shoulders. "My cousin Liza Bandon lives here. I think she's in trouble. Is that why you're here?"

He glanced around. "No. A Grayson Shield called. He reported that people have been in and out of this apartment all day."

I knitted my brows. "Did he say if my cousin was one of those people?" Surely, he wouldn't report anything to the cops if Liza was here or if he thought she was in trouble.

"No. Do you know who tore up the place?"

"No clue."

The more the hours ticked by with no sign of Liza, the more my stomach knotted. "I was here earlier today… "

Hodge returned. "There's no blue Honda outside."

The blood drained from me. Stars coated my vision. *Don't panic. Riley probably sensed danger and took off. You did tell her to do that.*

"Did you notice a black SUV with two men in it parked outside?" I asked, holding my breath.

Hodge shook his head.

I had to be as pale as the walls in the apartment. *First Liza. Now Riley.* Liza's last words were "take care of Riley." My heart skipped a beat. The cuffs were cutting off my circulation. And suddenly, the room was becoming claustrophobic. "Please take these cuffs off." My tone was lethal.

Tanner's eyebrows climbed to his dark hairline. "It's time to take you down to the station for more questioning."

"I need to find my girl." I did everything I could to soften my tone, but I knew firsthand that appealing to a cop never worked. I could talk until I was blue in the face. They were only doing their jobs. Case in point: Dad had called me to tell me Mom was in the hospital and that he didn't have good news.

"Get here as fast as you can," he'd said.

I'd explained to the officer that night that I was headed to an emergency.

"As much as I would like to believe you, I get that excuse all the time," the officer had said.

But a speeding ticket had a lower penalty than breaking and entering.

Tanner gripped my arm. "Let's go."

"Please. Can I at least call my girl?" I pleaded one more time.

"You'll get your phone call down at the station," Tanner said.

As soon as we were outside, my head darted to where Riley had been parked, but there was no car. I searched up and down the street to no avail. Even the black SUV was gone.

11

RILEY

I knew what I was doing was crazy and dangerous, but I had to follow the black SUV. The car had taken off about a minute after Josh had gone into Liza's apartment. I figured I could find out where they were going before Josh came out.

I wasn't an expert on how to follow someone, but at that point, I didn't care. All I wanted to do was find my friend, even if that meant the two men were leading me into a trap. Maybe then I would find Liza.

I was three cars behind the black SUV on a narrow city street that was as steep as a roller coaster, with the bay in the distance. The sun was setting, and if it weren't for the pretty scenery, I would've probably puked from the way my stomach pitched and rolled. I kept pumping the brakes as I made my way down the hill.

Charlie sat in the back seat, seemingly enjoying himself.

The SUV turned left just as the light changed to red.

I banged on the steering wheel as I came to a complete stop. Suddenly, I wanted to cry. Liza was missing. I felt helpless, and I had no idea where I was or if Liza was all right.

After what seemed like hours, the light finally changed, and I blew out a breath, staving off the tears that were ready to spill if someone looked at me the wrong way. When I made a left on Geary, the black SUV was nowhere in sight. Tears streamed out, hot and fast. My stomach was ready to heave the coffee I'd had that morning. Now that I was thinking about it, I hadn't eaten all day.

I felt as if I were in a time warp or a bad movie. I pulled over into a spot in front of a coffee shop. Charlie stuck his head in between the seats and panted in my ear. I reached around and scratched his jaw. Then he licked my face. As if that were all I needed, I giggled through tears.

"Thank you," I said to him. "We should call Josh."

At the mention of his name, Charlie barked.

The line went to voice mail. I redialed. Again, no luck. Maybe Liza's place didn't get great cell service.

"Josh, I'm sorry, but I had to follow the black SUV, only I lost them. I'm headed back to Liza's to pick you up."

I typed Liza's address into the navigation system in the car. I was about to merge into traffic when my phone rang.

"Riley," Josh said, sounding relieved. "You're all right."

"I'm fine. I'm lost, but good. Charlie is fine too. I'm sorry, but I wanted to follow the SUV. I lost them, though. Any luck on Liza?" I didn't think she was at her apartment like Taylor had said.

"No, but I need you to come down to the San Francisco police station and pick me up. I'll explain when you get here."

It took me over an hour to get to the other side of the city. I wasn't a great driver, even though I lived in one of the busiest cities in North America. I mainly took the train in and around Boston, although my job as a wedding planner had me traveling to the suburbs, which I always dreaded because of rush-hour traffic.

Construction plagued me through several streets with red lights and stop signs. The sea of pedestrians gave me a warm feeling that I was home despite the steep hills that were making me woozy.

Once I finally found the police station, it took me another twenty minutes to find a parking spot. By the time I walked into the station, my nerves were fried to a crisp.

Josh was waiting for me in the lobby, and wow! I wanted to run and jump into his muscular arms, kiss his thick lips, stare into his forest-green eyes, and run my hands through his sandy-blond hair. More than anything, I just wanted to feel his arms around me and have him tell me everything would be okay, and that we would find Liza alive and well.

But my vision of him embracing me was shattered when Charlie wagged his tail and ran to his owner. Josh squatted down and greeted him, peppering kisses all over Charlie's ears and nose.

Please do that to me. What I wouldn't have given to have that kind of attention.

As if the universe had heard me, Josh rose, smiled so wide that my heart jumped a mile, and swaggered over to me.

I clasped my hands in front of me so he wouldn't see that I was shaking. Then his large palm landed on my cheek. He leaned in and whispered in my ear. "Thank God nothing happened to you." He sounded as though he would've died if something had.

On that thought, I melted into a puddle of water. I'd only been in California for twenty-four hours, and my life had changed drastically. I was afraid when my vacation was over, I would turn into a pumpkin. I wasn't living the life of Cinderella with Liza missing, but Josh was definitely treating me as if I were a delicate flower, and I was absorbing every moment in his presence.

He edged back. "Now, about you taking off to follow that car. That wasn't the smartest thing to do."

I wasn't about to argue. It was stupid on my part because I had no idea what I would've done if they'd led me into a trap. "Were you arrested?"

"No. The cops showed up and thought I broke into Liza's. But they cleared me. I also filed a missing person's report. They have my contact info. So they'll call if they come up with anything." He grabbed Charlie's leash then wrapped his arm around me. "I think it's time we relax for the night."

I wasn't sure I could relax or sleep. I had to do something to search for Liza. But what? That was the million-dollar question.

We walked out as the city lights brightened and the sky darkened. A chill hung in the air, and I shivered.

Josh pulled me tighter to him.

I snuggled as much as I could against his rock-hard body, inhaling his masculine scent and enjoying the hold he had on me. I felt protected, and like I wasn't alone on this crazy roller-coaster ride. Despite my worry for Liza, I was beginning to feel something for Josh. If I were being honest with myself, I was both scared and excited. I did want to settle down and have kids. I did want someone like Josh, who was caring and a gentleman. I also wanted a man who was accepting of me, flaws and all. I felt as though Josh could be that guy.

But. There was always a but. I wasn't ready to get my heart broken again. Not that Josh gave me any vibes he was a cheater. It was more the long distance between us that would cause the damage.

I was getting way ahead of myself. I had a best friend to find first. "There's got to be something we could do to find Liza."

"Rest is the best thing right now. Otherwise, we won't be worth much if we're tired. I have to check on my dad too."

My heart broke at the mention of his dad. I'd had a chance to talk to him the night before. He'd shared with me that he was diagnosed with ALS shortly after his wife died, and each day since, he'd lost more and more of his ability to hold a cup, help himself up out of his wheelchair, and even eat.

Josh and I strolled to the car that I'd parked a block from the station.

"Do you think a room at the inn might be available tonight for me?" I'd intruded enough on him and his father.

"Not cool on staying with my dad and me?" he asked in a playful tone, but underneath I got the impression he was disappointed.

When we got to the car, I handed him the keys. "With the time change, I would only be up early, and I don't want to wake anyone."

"We're booked solid. I doubt we'll have a room."

Maybe it was best to stay with Josh and his dad. At least they would keep me company and get my mind off of Liza.

12

JOSH

The weekend came and went with no sign of Liza. The SFPD didn't have any leads either. Riley and I checked in with Taylor several times, but she hadn't heard from Liza since Friday, which was four days ago, the day the cops had dragged me down to the station. I had racked my brain since we'd questioned Taylor, trying to remember if Liza had ever mentioned anything about her former employer or anyone she'd dealt with recently that might have frightened her. But I had nothing.

Riley had to extend her trip. She didn't want to leave until she knew Liza was safe.

I waltzed into the restaurant at the inn. Riley had found a corner table near the window that overlooked the Pacific. Her black-as-night hair was tied up on top of her head. Gold-hoop earrings dangled from her ears, and her long neck appeared smooth as silk. I itched to drag my fingers over her skin.

I slid into the chair across from her.

She typed furiously on her laptop, completely absorbed in what she was doing.

I cleared my throat. "I think it's time you take a break."

She'd been working nonstop on her computer for two days in

between helping me with my dad. I had protested that she didn't need to do anything around the house, but she'd insisted.

"If I'm going to stay with you, I need to earn my keep, and helping takes my mind off of Liza," she'd said.

Dad was loving the fact that we had a lady in the house, and one he was trying every which way to set me up with. I couldn't blame him. Secretly, I wanted him to do what he could, like put in a good word for me with Riley, although I had a feeling he didn't have to do that.

I'd found her stealing looks at me in the mornings when I walked into the kitchen. I would do the same to her when she wasn't looking. She seemed so at ease and at home around the house. It was as though she belonged there.

Stop getting ahead of yourself.

The only good thing about Liza missing was that I got to spend time with Riley and learn her little quirks, like when she stirred sugar in her coffee, she went clockwise and then counterclockwise before setting down the spoon. Or she tugged on her earlobe when she was telling me about how she and Liza had often talked about opening up a dress shop together where Liza would design dresses, wedding ones in particular.

Aside from all that, my stomach tumbled endlessly anytime I was around her like at that moment. As I stared into her luscious gray eyes, they mesmerized me.

She stopped typing. "I might have to fly back to Boston. I don't want to, but the longer I stay, the more behind I'll get, and then I'll have some angry clients."

"I'll call the SFPD again today. Maybe we should talk to Grayson, Liza's neighbor, to see if he's heard any more activity in her apartment." I had no doubt that if Liza were home, she would've called or even shown up at the inn like she had been scheduled to the week before. "For now, let's go for a walk. Drake has things covered here. My dad is taking a nap in between watching Netflix."

She sighed. "I could use a break." Suddenly, a tear trickled down her cheek.

I reached over and grasped her cold hand. "Hey, we'll find Liza." I wasn't so sure about that, but the only conclusion I could come up with was that Liza hadn't been kidnapped by Moretti's men, not if they were stalking her apartment.

Riley squeezed my fingers. "I can't imagine what has happened to her. I keep going over it in my head. My brother, Ross, tells me that Stefano's arraignment is tomorrow. I can't help but think that maybe Stefano is trying to shut up all his employees, past and present, until his trial is over. I mean, if no one testifies against him, then there isn't a case."

"That would depend," I said, "on what kind of evidence the law has. They may not need anyone to testify."

She flicked a button on her computer then began reading. "It says here that Stefano's lawyer believes the prosecution has nothing on his client."

I pushed to my feet then circled the table and grabbed the back of her chair. "Come on. A break will do you good. Charlie could use a walk as well."

She didn't protest as she closed her computer.

After I grabbed Charlie, the three of us strolled down Main Street, passing stores and other establishments.

The air was cool. The sun was shining, and tourists were window-shopping like we were, or like Riley was.

A bridal shop had caught her attention, one that was for sale.

Charlie sniffed around one of the many pear trees on the street. I tugged lightly on his leash, then joined Riley. A mannequin stood tall inside the window, wearing an off-the-shoulder cream-colored wedding dress.

Riley hooked her arm around mine. "I noticed the inn hosts weddings."

"We have. We don't do many. When my mom was alive, we did more."

She stared at the window, her mind so far away.

A group of bikers pedaled by. Cars passed slowly.

Before I knew what was happening, Riley's small, cold hand was clutching mine. "If you don't mind me asking, what happened to your mom?"

I glanced at our connection and swallowed hard, mainly because I wanted her so badly, not because she'd brought up my mom. I thought about Mom all the time, especially when I saw a bride. My mom loved weddings.

"Shortly after I was discharged from the Navy, she was diagnosed with pancreatic cancer. She died shortly after she found out."

Riley squeezed my hand as we both fixated on the wedding dress. "I'm sorry for your loss."

A pain gripped my chest. Dad and I hardly spoke of Mom. It was still too painful for both of us. But holding Riley's hand seemed to ease the pain.

"I don't know how long I can stay, but if you need my help or advice on wedding planning for one of your guests, I would be happy to chip in."

I kissed the back of her hand. "Thank you."

She blushed as she pointed at the For Sale sign in the window. "Do you know why the shop is for sale?"

"Business has been slow for the owners. Actually, since we cut back on weddings at the inn, we haven't had the draw in town. The big tourist attractions are hikes into the redwoods, whale watching, fishing, and outdoor sports like zip-lining."

She lifted up on her toes, pressed her lips to my good ear, and whispered, "This would be a great place to open up a dress shop." Her tone was excited and sultry, and because of that, an inferno lit inside me.

I was about to do something I'd been dying to do since she had walked into the inn—kiss her deeply and passionately. But Charlie nudged my free hand, breaking the hold Riley had over me.

"A man is saying hi to Charlie," Riley said.

I turned and found Dr. Keller, the town veterinarian and Charlie's doctor, waving at us as he hurried into Sweets and Treats, the local bakery that served delectables for both humans and dogs.

I returned the wave, then gave Riley my full attention again. I didn't kiss her because the spark had died for the moment, although

I was a million percent sure the need to pepper kisses up and down her beautiful neck, face, and body would hit me hard again.

But right then, I had a burning question for her. "Back to the bridal shop. Are you saying you would move to California?" *Please say yes.*

She gave me the most heart-stopping smile. "Maybe."

I would take a maybe. Maybes were good. No, they were great. This called for a celebration. The sign for Cup of Joe's poked out in the distance. "There's a diner down the street that has some good coffee. Why don't we grab a cup, and I'll fill you in on Redwood Cove and what we have to offer."

She giggled. "You like that I would move here."

Like wasn't the word I would use. "Might as well have all your facts to be able to make a decision."

"I only need one fact."

I cocked an eyebrow when my phone vibrated against my leg. I was tempted to drop the nuisance piece of metal into the trash can, but it could be the SFPD. I dug the phone out of my pocket and answered it.

"Josh. Oh my God." Taylor sounded rattled. "Two men from Boston were here, asking for Liza. They're with the FBI. I told them you were looking for her too. They're on their way to see you."

"Did they tell you anything? Why they wanted to talk to Liza?"

"No. The only thing they said was that she could be in danger and to call them if I hear from Liza. I'm scared, Josh."

The woman was frightened for sure. Yet something was bothering me. "Did you lie to Riley and me about talking to Liza that day we were at your place?"

She was breathing heavily, as though she'd been running. "I promise I told you the truth." Taylor didn't strike me as the type to be involved in anything bad.

"Did the FBI say when they would be here?"

Riley's jaw came unhinged.

"They left the office well over an hour ago."

Depending on traffic, they could've been at the inn as we spoke.

13

RILEY

W e jogged back to the inn, my heart racing, my body sweating, and my mind sifting through all the scenarios of why the FBI was looking for Liza. There was no doubt she was in danger. I could feel that in my bones.

Regardless, I was fighting with one thing at the moment, and I wanted to laugh at myself. I was so out of shape. I wasn't fat, but I wasn't thin either. Like any woman, I was critical of my body. If there were one physical attribute I could've changed about myself, it would've been my stomach. I was always envious of Liza, who could eat anything and have a flat stomach. But if I even looked at chocolate, my stomach seemed to grow. Despite my hang-ups, I was thankful I was wearing flats and not heels.

By the time we reached the parking lot of the inn, I bent over to catch my breath. Josh and Charlie didn't even seem to be panting. I made a mental note to start back on my treadmill when I returned home to get my heart in shape if for nothing else.

Maybe I could start walking in the mornings while I was in California. Josh's dad had mentioned something about a cliff walk not too far from town that had awesome views of the Pacific, along with beautiful homes. I was more interested in taking a hike through the redwoods, but I hadn't brought my hiking boots or sneakers with me.

There's a sports store in town. Just buy a pair. You make good money.

On my last intake of crisp air, Josh laid a hand on my back and rubbed. Immediately, my body rioted with tingles. "Are you all right?"

Keep rubbing, and I will be. "It seems I need to get back on my workout schedule." I straightened, and then his touch was gone. I almost pouted.

"Stay with me long enough, and I'll get you in shape. Not that you're out of shape," he was quick to add as he combed rugged fingers through his thick hair.

I wanted to run my fingers through that hair.

Stop torturing yourself and do something. You're two consenting adults.

I let out a flirty laugh at my inner thoughts as I admired how boyish he appeared when he corrected himself. Then, as quickly as he'd flashed those forest-green eyes, he schooled his features and became Josh, the Navy SEAL, scanning the lot and looking at every car as though he sensed an immediate threat. "I don't see any black SUV."

I redid my messy bun. "Did Taylor say the FBI was driving a black SUV?"

He shook his head. "Come to think of it, no."

A blue four-door sedan wheeled into the lot and stopped underneath the portico that led to the main entrance.

I pointed to the car. "Maybe they're the FBI?"

A tall man and a short man got out of the car. A valet greeted the tall man, who was the driver. Both wore business suits, which didn't scream tourists.

Josh grasped my sweaty hand. "Let's find out."

Holding hands was becoming the norm for us, and I wasn't complaining. I loved that we had fallen into a somewhat comfortable friendship. Maybe by the time I left California, we would be more than friends.

Kiss Josh again and you might find out.

Actually, his dad was hoping for the same. "Josh is a good man who needs a good woman like you," his dad had blatantly said.

I'd had no comeback for that except to agree with the Josh lookalike.

We walked into the Redwood Cove Inn behind the two suits, who stopped to talk to Drake at the front desk.

Drake, who I was finding adored Liza, had his cell phone to his ear until he saw Josh. Then he shifted his dark gaze between the men and Josh, trying to tell him the men were there to see him.

Subtlety wasn't Drake's strong suit. The men caught on quickly, as they both turned.

The tall man, who had chestnut-colored eyes, pulled out a wallet from the inside of his suit jacket. "Josh Bandon? I'm Special Agent Wallace with the FBI." He flashed his credentials, then stabbed a thumb at his partner. "This is Special Agent Dennison. Can we talk?"

Soft music played overhead in the lobby. A boy who looked to be about three whined to his mom as they came toward us.

Josh angled his right side at Wallace. "I'm sorry. I didn't catch your name. I'm hearing impaired."

Wallace glanced down at Charlie, who was staring up at the men. "Oh. Wallace and Dennison," Wallace practically shouted.

I would imagine Josh would've heard them fine if it weren't for the cranky boy and other noises in the lobby. He'd also said he was good at reading lips, but the mom and boy had cut a path in between the four of us, apologizing for the intrusion as she and her boy left the inn.

"This is Riley and my dog Charlie. Let me get Charlie settled. Can you meet us in the restaurant?" Josh waved a hand straight ahead.

The agents took their leave.

While Josh escorted Charlie to his dog bed, I ducked into the ladies' room. I needed to splash cold water on my face to calm the nervous nellies eating my stomach alive. I was eager to hear what the FBI had to say; yet I was afraid they had bad news.

They hadn't told Taylor anything bad had happened to Liza.

Taylor wasn't family, though, and Josh was. I was assuming too much. It was so like me to think the worst.

I inhaled deeply, going through some quick meditation techniques. I always loved to meditate in the confines of my living room, which had an incredible view of Boston, although I was quickly changing my tune about city life. The ocean and the small town of Redwood were growing on me fast.

With one last deep breath, I coated my face with water, patted it dry with a paper towel, and deposited the towel in the trash.

The door squeaked open.

"Riley." Josh's husky voice echoed in the sterile room. "Are you in here?"

I giggled. His voice was like warm butter, melting me in all the right places. Yeah, I was falling for him, and if he kept holding my hand and touching me, his dad might get his wish.

As soon as I met Josh in the lobby, he cupped my elbow. Always the gentleman, I was finding.

Wallace and Dennison were drinking coffee at the table I had commandeered for the last few days in a quiet corner of the restaurant that had a breathtaking view of the ocean. It was mid-afternoon, so only a patron or two hung out at the bar, watching a baseball game on the big-screen TV.

Both agents rose when they laid eyes on me. Josh pulled out a chair next to Wallace, the tall agent whose dark hair was cut thick on top and shaved on the sides and back, much like Josh's. Dennison, on the other hand, had wavy reddish-orange hair that curled around his ears.

As Josh eased down into the chair across from me, he said, "Riley is my cousin Liza's best friend, and she's in town from Boston. I hope you don't mind if she joins us. That is, if you're here to ask about Liza Bandon."

Dennison had his coffee cup to his lips. "We are. And we're hoping you can answer some questions."

Sadly, we didn't have much to tell them.

Wallace started in. "We're from the Boston office. Do either of you know where Liza is?"

I let out a nervous laugh. "I was hoping you could tell us."

"The last we both heard from Liza"—Josh wagged a finger between him and me—"was last Thursday evening. When I spoke to her, she sounded like something was bothering her. I chalked it up to her working late, which she's been known to do."

"She sounded tired to me," I added. "And she and I were supposed to spend a few days together. I'm worried out of my mind. So are you here because of Stefano Moretti?"

Wallace glanced at his partner, but I couldn't tell if he was trying to mind-speak or not. Then he took a sip of his coffee. "I've been working on the Moretti case for over two years. I was the one who questioned Liza after the raid on his company. Back then, she didn't have much to tell us, and we hadn't been able to find any evidence to hold Moretti on anything then. But over a week ago, right before Moretti was arrested again, she left me a message and said she needed to talk, and that it was urgent. I've tried to reach her, but she's either had a change of heart, or someone spooked her."

"Do you have any idea what she wanted to talk about?" Josh asked.

Wallace bit the inside of his cheek. "I wish I did. I'm speculating, though, that she has some information on Moretti. Whether it's new or old, I don't know."

"So you think she's still in contact with Moretti?" I doubted it.

"Maybe, or maybe someone else who works for him," Dennison piped in.

I held one of my nails hostage between my teeth. "If it helps, Liza still talks to a gal by the name of Haley, who worked or maybe still works for Moretti."

Dennison jotted down some notes on a pad he'd removed from his suit pocket.

Josh rubbed his stubbled jaw. "One of the notes on Liza's desk was to call Haley and you." He nodded at Wallace.

Maybe the puzzle pieces were falling into place, but I didn't know how yet. It was looking as though Liza had some information to share with the FBI, or maybe Haley did. Come to think of it, maybe Haley was the woman Grayson had heard that night from his bedroom balcony.

"Do you have a last name?" Dennison asked.

I thought back to conversations I'd had with Liza, but she hadn't mentioned a surname. "I don't."

"Liza's neighbor overheard Liza and a girl arguing," Josh said. "Maybe that person was Haley. And Liza's apartment was ransacked. I'm not a detective, but it seems someone is looking for something."

Liza could've been exchanging heated words with Taylor rather than Haley, although Taylor hadn't mentioned anything of the sort.

Yeah, but you think she's hiding something. So she wouldn't tell you.

Both agents whipped their heads at Josh.

Dennison set down his pen. "Wallace, you always suspected Liza was holding something back on Moretti."

Josh's eyebrows drew down. "Like what?"

This I had to hear. Liza had sworn she didn't have a darn thing bad to say about Moretti. Maybe she was frightened that if she had said something negative, he would've had one of his men kill her. After all, she'd told me the whole interrogation process had been nerve-racking.

"Hunch," Wallace replied. "Liza was nervous when I talked to her, and she kept looking over her shoulder as though someone was nearby listening to her."

Wallace appeared to be an experienced agent, given his forty-something age. I would guess that with his tenure, he had seen a ton of crime. Dennison, on the other hand, appeared to be much younger. Still, experience was one thing; intuition was another. I always tried to follow mine.

"We were at her apartment a few days ago and found a black SUV with two men watching her place," I said. "I even followed them but lost them in the city. I'm assuming they're Moretti's men trying to keep Liza from testifying at his hearing."

Dennison narrowed his eyes at me, reminding me of my brother when I did something Ross didn't like.

I raised my hands off the table a little. "I know. Stupid move.

But if it led me to my best friend, then I would've called the cops before doing anything dangerous." At least I hoped that I would have. I'd always been the curious one out of Ross and me. I was the twin who took chances no matter the danger. A good example was when my cell phone had fallen into the Boston Harbor. I'd been ready to dive in if my brother hadn't stopped me. But life and work had been on that phone. "Think before you do something" were my brother's famous words.

Dennison's pen was poised to write. "Did you get a look at the people inside the SUV?"

"Barely," I said. "The windows were tinted. But the driver might've had dark hair. They took off so fast." Plus, I was trying to look inconspicuous.

Wallace was still gnawing on the inside of his cheek. "We've had surveillance on all of Moretti's men, and none of them have left Boston. But maybe a couple slipped by. I'll double-check. We'll see if we can find a Haley that worked for Moretti. I questioned a lot of people the day of the raid, but I don't recall a Haley."

Then it dawned on me. If Moretti's men were looking for Liza, that meant they hadn't kidnapped her. Suddenly, I wanted to kick myself in the butt for not connecting those dots. For all we knew, Liza had gotten into an accident. After all, she'd been in a rush to meet me. She could be laid up in a hospital somewhere.

14

JOSH

R iley had her lips mashed together as though she were thinking extremely hard.

Grinning, I slid a hand over the table. She looked adorable with her nose wrinkled. "What is it?" I reached for her, when she brought her fingers up to her mouth.

"Remember Taylor said that Liza was in a hurry because she was late to meet me?" She held a nail between her teeth. "We should check the hospitals."

My stomach plummeted. We'd been so caught up in Taylor and mafia men that I hadn't even thought about the possibility that Liza could be hurt.

"We're one step ahead of you," Dennison said. "We have our team checking with local law enforcement as well as hospitals in the city. We decided to take the step after speaking with Taylor Manning."

Riley sagged in her chair. I sighed as my mind rioted on one thing. Maybe the two men who had shown up to see Liza the previous week were with the FBI too. Wallace had said that none of Moretti's men had left Boston.

"Are any of your colleagues here from Boston?" I asked. "And how long have you guys been in town?"

Dennison regarded me. "We flew in earlier today. And we're the only two agents here from Boston."

There went my theory. I stared down at the wooden table before regarding Wallace. "Taylor mentioned to us that the men who had shown up at her office, asking for Liza, said they were friends of Liza's."

Wallace bobbed his head. "We know. Taylor told us. She also gave us their descriptions. We questioned others at Stitches, but no one could tell us anything, although we haven't talked to Liza's boss. He wasn't there."

Maybe Riley was wrong about Taylor hiding something.

"We have to check in with our team." Wallace pulled out a business card. "Call me if you think of anything else or hear from Liza. In the meantime, are there any rooms available here for the night?"

Since it was midweek, we should've had some availability. "I'll check." I pushed to my feet.

Riley popped up too, when her phone rang.

I held my breath, hoping it was Liza.

"My brother," she said. "Sorry, I have to take this." She sashayed out of the restaurant and into the lobby.

I tapped on the table. "Hang tight. I'll be right back." I wound my way around empty tables, passing a couple of waiters who were setting up for the dinner crowd.

Once I reached the lobby, Charlie trotted up, wagging his tail. At the same time, my dad wheeled out from the office that was located around the corner from the front desk.

"Son, what's going on?" My dad's voice was so loud, it echoed in the small hallway where the office and restrooms were located.

I held up a finger, motioning for my dad to hold on. "Drake, can you set up the agents with two rooms?"

He nodded his bald head as he went to work, tapping on keys.

I tipped my head to the office. "Come on, Dad." I didn't want anyone in the lobby to hear our conversation, and in the confines of the office, I could hear Dad a little clearer, and he wouldn't have to shout.

Charlie followed Dad and me inside, then hopped up on the loveseat that banked the side wall. The office was a modest size with the essential desk, chair, and filing cabinets. At times, the space was claustrophobic for me, especially after I closed the door.

Dad wheeled over and parked himself behind the desk. "Son, tell me everything."

I began pacing, wearing a hole in the carpet on the other side of Dad.

I didn't want to burden my dad with what-ifs or speculate. He'd been through enough with his ALS and the loss of my mom. I didn't want him worrying over Liza, who was like a daughter to him.

A knock sounded, then the door opened, and Riley poked her head in.

Man, she was a sight for sore eyes, even though we hadn't been separated but five minutes. I waved her in and had the urge to pull her to me, wrap my arms around her, and inhale her fruity scent.

She gave me one of her groin-tightening smiles. "I hope I'm not interrupting."

"Of course not," Dad said.

Riley skirted the desk and kissed Dad on the cheek.

I wanted to ask where my kiss was.

Dad's face lit up like a Christmas tree.

The two were becoming quite close, which was good and bad— good in the sense that they were bonding, but bad in the sense that he would be heartbroken when she returned to Boston. I knew he was doing his best to push us toward being a couple, getting married, and the whole nine yards.

Hell, I wanted her to stay too. I wanted her around perma- nently. But my relationship status would have to wait. We needed to find Liza.

Riley eased down on the cushion next to Charlie. "It sounds like Taylor has been telling us the truth, but I still claim she's hiding something about Liza, mainly because she seemed too nervous when we met her at her apartment. I might be wrong, but I don't think Liza called her that day and said she was on her way to her apartment. If Liza had been, she would've called us, Josh."

Riley was right. Why would Liza talk to Taylor and not us, especially Riley, since the two had plans together?

"Are you two going to share?" Dad asked.

Riley and I filled him in on the conversation we'd had with the agents, including how Liza could've been hurt and in a hospital in the city.

Dad shook his graying-blond head of hair. "She would've called if she was in a hospital, or at least someone would've called us or her father." He lifted the receiver of the desk phone. "I'll call my brother."

I doubted Liza would've had anyone call her old man. If I had to wager, I doubted Liza carried his phone number in her purse.

I sighed as I sat down on the arm of the loveseat with Riley next to me.

Riley rubbed Charlie's back as he laid his head on a pillow. "I know you said rent is expensive in the city, but I can't help but think that something isn't right with Taylor. She's dressed as though she comes from money. The ring on her finger is evidence that at least her fiancé has money, and the rundown apartment doesn't match up with her persona."

I couldn't say I disagreed, but that dinky and dingy apartment probably rented for at least fifteen hundred dollars a month.

"I'm going into the city first thing in the morning to talk to Taylor," Riley said as sure as Charlie was snoring.

I jerked so hard, I almost fell on top of her. *Over my dead body.* "You're not going alone."

You can't stop her. You don't have any say in what she does. And let's not forget you're handicapped. With your slight limp and lack of hearing, you wouldn't even hear a gun being cocked until it was too late.

Dad set the receiver down. "No answer. Also, I have my quarterly appointment with my neurologist tomorrow at Gold Coast General."

"Then we'll go after your appointment." I could make arrangements for one of his caregivers to take him, but I wanted to be with him. That way, I could hear firsthand what the doctor had to say, especially if we had to make decisions on the next steps of my dad's medical care. His neurologist had recommended a feeding tube at some point. Dad wasn't quite there yet, but he was starting to have problems with swallowing.

Riley rested a hand on my thigh. "You take care of your dad. I'll be fine. I'm just going to talk to Taylor. Besides, she might open up to me without you there. I think she's afraid of you."

I pushed my tongue against my teeth to keep from groaning at how good her hand felt on me. Maybe I was exaggerating a little on how she affected me, but the woman had some kind of hold over my mind and body.

"And what if the black SUV shows up? Or they follow you this time?"

The more Charlie got rubbed, the more I pouted, wishing I were a dog. *How crazy is that?*

"They don't know who I am."

"So those men didn't see you in the car as they passed by?"

"Maybe. But I was petting Charlie when they drove by, which was another reason I didn't get a good look. I was trying not to bring attention to myself. Besides, they probably didn't even think twice about a girl and her dog. I promise I'll call you as soon as I'm done and on my way back here."

I studied her and realized she had a beauty mark just below her left eye.

My dad cleared his throat, bringing me out of my lust-filled haze.

Focus, man.

A wild laugh broke out in my head. As long as Riley was near me, my head would be fuzzy.

Both Dad and Riley said my name at the same time.

I blinked and found my dad grinning, as though he knew what I was thinking. He probably did since he was a man too.

"Promise you'll call me as soon as you leave the city," I said to Riley, knowing deep down in my gut that I was going to regret not going with her.

15

RILEY

The drive into the city was horrible. Boston had traffic, but not like the Bay Area. The cars were backed up for miles on the Golden Gate Bridge.

Josh had said rush hour started at five in the morning and that by nine, most commuters were at their desks.

The clock in the car read 9:15 a.m. He'd been so wrong.

Maybe summer vacation was responsible for all the traffic. My GPS indicated that I had thirty minutes to my destination, which was a short five miles away.

Taking in a much-needed breath, I gripped the steering wheel as I hit the gas, only to move an inch before I pumped the brakes. It had been like that for the last forty minutes.

Traffic was the bane of my existence. Maybe I should find a place in the country, away from the bustle of the city—any city.

You love the energy, the atmosphere, and the fast-paced city life. I'd grown up listening to horns blowing outside my bedroom window and the noise of engines purring at all hours of the night.

The marine layer hovered over the city in the distance, and the temperature was a cool fifty-five degrees. I pushed the down button to crack a window, then closed it quickly when too much exhaust from the cars suddenly filtered in.

I had plenty of time to think about what I would ask Taylor, and the more I noodled on everything the woman had told us, the more something bothered me. She hadn't sounded as concerned as we were about Liza. To me, it almost sounded as though she knew Liza was fine. I wasn't holding out hope that Taylor would tell me anything. But if she was being loyal to Liza, then I couldn't fault her for that. But by golly, if Taylor knew anything, I would do my best to yank it out of her.

I pumped the brake when my phone rang and shut down the radio. Then I hit the connect button.

"Riley, it's Josh. Did you make it?"

I giggled. "Um, no. I'm sitting on the bridge in traffic. You're worried about me, aren't you?"

Quietness ticked over the line. I had to look at the screen then my phone to see if we'd gotten disconnected. "Josh, are you there?"

"Yes, I'm worried. I hate that you're doing this alone."

I warmed at the knowledge that Josh was worried about me. But I couldn't sit around anymore and wait for information on Liza.

"What time is your dad's appointment?" Maybe I could take his mind off of me.

"In about an hour. But I want you to call me after you speak with Taylor." His voice was deep and husky, causing the butterflies in my stomach to take flight. He also sounded as if he were the leader of an army. I imagined some of his Navy SEAL training was idling on the surface, waiting to come out and take charge.

"Yes, sir," I teased.

"And Riley," he said softly that time. "After we find Liza, would you like to get dinner and go to a movie?"

Those butterflies fluttering around in my belly went wild. I wanted to blurt out "yes, yes, yes." But a little voice in the back of my mind was cautioning me. I had to get back to Boston and my job soon. I wasn't sure how much longer I could stay. My assistants were doing a great job filling in for me, but they could only do so much for so long. Moreover, we had the wedding of all weddings coming up in about a month. The mayor of Boston's daughter was getting married. I'd been fortunate to secure that contract two years ago. I had to be there, and not just for the wedding day. The two weeks prior to a wedding were always an extremely busy time to get every detail ready for the big day.

"Can we find Liza and then talk?" He had to know that I was returning to Boston.

Silence ticked—one second then two. "Sure." Disappointment laced his tone. "My dad is calling me. Talk soon." Then the music filled the car.

The last thing I wanted to do was hurt Josh or get hurt myself.

One date doesn't mean marriage. Maybe not, but it could lead to feelings that we couldn't explore if we were on opposite ends of the country.

I tuned in to the radio as I inched another foot. I couldn't think about my love life, so instead, I ran through some questions in my head that I would ask Taylor when I arrived.

After forty-five minutes, I was walking into Stitches Incorporated. My body was tense from the stop-and-go traffic. It didn't help that I'd been gripping the wheel so tightly, I thought my fingers were going to fall off.

Candace, the receptionist who'd caught Josh in Liza's office, was sitting at the reception desk. When she lifted her blue eyes and found me, she winced. Then a scowl formed.

I imagined Taylor had reprimanded her or told on her. Either way, I didn't regret what Josh and I had done. I would've done anything to find my best friend.

Candace stood up, smoothing a hand down her soft, gray, sleeveless dress. "Liza isn't here." Her lips were pursed so tightly that her red lipstick cracked.

I gave her one of my fake business smiles that I painted on when I met clients. As a professional, it was polite to put on that happy face. "I would like to see Taylor Manning."

She pinned me with a glare. "You don't have an appointment."

I lost my smile. I thought Candace and I had bonded a smidge the other day. Then again, if she'd gotten into trouble for giving us Taylor's address, any connection I'd made was gone.

In our previous conversation, Candace had shared with me that she was engaged. I wasn't into bribing people, but the circumstances called for extreme measures. I dipped into my purse and produced a business card. "I'm sorry if you got into trouble because of me. But I would like to make it up to you." I handed her my card. "I can give you a discount on a cake for your wedding or even cut you a deal on the cost of the venue."

She read the card, pinching her perfectly manicured eyebrows. "This says Boston on it. I'm getting married in San Francisco. Do you have an office out here?"

I tucked hair behind my ear. I'd left my hair down instead of twisting it up on my head that day. "I work with a lot of companies outside of the New England area." I didn't do business with anyone in California. Yet if she told me where she was having her reception or who was making her cake, I would pay ten percent of her bill, which could be significant if she chose to take me up on my offer.

She blew out a breath. "I don't take bribes."

The fifteenth floor of executive offices was as quiet as it had been the other day when I'd visited. I wondered for a split second if people actually worked on that floor.

"It's my way of saying I'm sorry."

She studied me for a second before she said, "You're lucky I didn't lose my job."

I was curious as to what she would've done to me if she had lost her job. She didn't strike me as the type to take revenge on anyone. In fact, she came across as fragile and desperate.

I leaned onto the counter. "Look, Candace, I don't want any trouble. I know Liza isn't here. I need to talk to Taylor. She might know where Liza is." My tone was low and soft. "I need to find my best friend. Her family is quite worried too. Wouldn't you do anything if something happened to a loved one?"

The area around her eyes crinkled. "I would call the cops."

I held back a snarl. "Sadly, we did. The SFPD doesn't have any leads to go on. The FBI doesn't either."

Her features softened as she sat down. "Taylor said she didn't want to be disturbed."

I figuratively scratched my head. Taylor was an assistant, not an executive of the company who could give that type of order.

"Then I'll wait," I said. "I'm not leaving here until I talk to Taylor."

Her chest lifted as she considered me. "Are you serious about a discount?"

I nodded.

She scraped her nails through her bright-red hair. "I could use a discount for the cake."

"Done. Now can you get Taylor?"

She lifted the phone's receiver and pushed a button. "Yes, Riley is here to see you." There was a brief pause. "Sure." She set down the phone. "Taylor is finishing up a call. She'll be here in a few minutes." Candace pocketed my card. "My wedding isn't for another two months. So I'll call you with the details of my cake."

"Great. It was a long drive in. Can I use the restroom while I wait? I know where it is." I didn't give her a chance to answer me. I seriously had to use the ladies' room.

On my way down the hall of offices, I could feel her watching me. When I reached the bathroom, I smiled her way before going in.

I quickly took care of business and had every intention of returning to the waiting area until I heard Taylor's voice coming from one of the offices. I checked for Candace, but she had stepped away.

Clutching the strap of my purse, I inched down the black-carpeted hall like a cat burglar, looking over my shoulder every few steps for Candace or security.

"Where are you?" Taylor asked.

I stopped outside Liza's office, then peeked in.

Taylor was at a glass desk with her back to me, facing the city view out the floor-to-ceiling window.

If I weren't mistaken, this was Liza's office. Or maybe it wasn't. When Candace had caught Josh the other day, Liza's office had racks of dresses hiding the furniture. This one had been cleared out as though Liza had been let go.

I scanned the hall and the doors. No nameplates existed on any of them. I should've knocked, but I wanted to eavesdrop some more.

However, I didn't get a chance to even take my next breath before Candace called my name rather loudly.

I almost cowered as if I'd been caught passing a note to my best friend in junior high. It had been an embarrassing day when Ms. Fennel had taken my note and read it to the class.

I made out with Daniel. He kisses sloppy.

The entire class had laughed as I'd turned a million shades of deep red.

Candace hurried down the hall and came to a full stop in front of me, planting her hands on her thin hips. "You don't belong down here. I should get security."

And I should've screamed at the top of my lungs. Why didn't anyone at this company care that Liza was missing?

So I mimicked her body language right down to the scowl on her face. "I think I'll call security. What don't you people understand? Liza Bandon is missing. I believe someone around here knows where she is."

A door popped open down a few yards from where I stood, and a chunky man with gray hair and a gray mustache walked out, wearing a sharp business suit. "What's going on?"

Taylor threw her door open, her blue eyes wide. "Nothing, Mr. Gansett." Her voice cracked.

"Bull," I said as I stalked up to Mr. Gansett.

He smoothed a hand down his blue tie as he hovered just outside his office.

Taylor rushed to my side and grabbed my arm, her nails digging into my skin. "I'll handle this, Mr. Gansett."

Candace joined us. "I'm sorry, sir."

Both Candace and Taylor were nervous, leading me to believe that this well-dressed man had some clout at the company.

I jerked out of Taylor's hold. "Touch me again, and I will give you the shiner of your life." I wasn't one to punch or physically fight. I left that to Ross, who always threw punches first then asked questions later. But I wasn't one to let people walk all over me or touch me like Taylor had. The last girl who'd pushed me in the schoolyard in the eighth grade had ended up with a bloody nose.

Mr. Gansett held up fat fingers. "Ladies, calm down. Candace, return to reception. Taylor, in my office."

Candace practically ran, as if Mr. Gansett would cut off her head… or fire her. Taylor, on the hand, sashayed into Mr. Gansett's office as though she weren't afraid of the man, which belied the fear in her voice.

"Now what's this about?" Mr. Gansett asked in a polite tone.

"I believe Taylor has information on the whereabouts of Liza Bandon."

He angled his head. "It is my understanding that Liza is away on a business trip."

I let out an evil laugh. It was clear to me that this man didn't know what was going on, or maybe he did and didn't care. But my intuition was telling me that he believed Liza was on a business trip.

"Look, Ms…"

"Lewis. I'm Riley Lewis."

He grinned as though something had dawned on him. "The wedding planner, Riley Lewis? As in the one planning the wedding for the Boston Mayor's daughter? Liza's best friend from Boston?" Awe washed over him as if I were some big celebrity.

Liza had screamed in excitement when I'd told her I got the contract of my career. I guessed she hadn't been able to contain how proud she was of me. Not that the news of my contract was a secret. In fact, the newspapers in Boston were all abuzz with speculation on the dress and the guest list, almost as if Brenda Nuñez, the soon-to-be Mrs. David Williams, were royalty.

The anger that had taken hold of my stomach weakened for the moment. "In the flesh."

"Why didn't you say so? I'm Liza's boss. She told me she would be spending time with you. Are you saying that didn't happen last weekend?" His bushy eyebrows rose slightly.

"The last time I heard from her was the day she was supposed to pick me up at the airport, which was almost a week ago now. Her family is as worried as I am. The FBI is looking for her too."

He flinched then waved a hand into his office. "Why don't you come in, and we'll get to the bottom of this."

Agent Wallace had said Liza's boss hadn't been in the office when he and Dennison questioned the employees.

I sighed quietly. Finally, someone wanted to help, someone who seemed to care about Liza's welfare.

16

JOSH

I transferred Dad from his wheelchair to his recliner in front of the TV in the family room. Our house was located on the same side of the street as the inn, which meant that my dad's property had a view of the Pacific, although the view wasn't as spectacular as the one from Redwood Cove Inn. Part of our view was obstructed by the cliffs off to the right.

Nevertheless, the family room had accordion glass doors that opened to a deck. I cracked open one side of the glass panel to let in the cool ocean air.

Dad flicked on the TV. "I just love when the breeze comes in."

I loved everything about living there. Memories of Mom accosted me every time I walked into the family room. I would always find her sitting in her chaise lounge, crocheting hats, scarves, and other items for the humanitarian group she belonged to at the local church.

I didn't think I would ever move. When my dad passed, I would inherit not only the house, but Redwood Cove Inn. I clutched the back of my neck and focused on the waves, trying not to think that far into the future. Losing my mom had been heart-wrenching. I didn't want to go through something like that again. Yet I knew that was a pipe dream.

Dad's neurologist couldn't give him an exact time on when his ALS would escalate. On average, people with ALS lasted three years from the time they were diagnosed. Dad was at the beginning of his second year. In addition, he was taking medication to slow the process. However, slowing down his ALS only meant he could tack on two or three months to his life.

The wind was playing with the waves, as was a surfer. I'd never had the itch to try surfing, although the guy appeared to be in his element and having a good time. My idea of a good time was strapping on my SEAL gear, hanging out with my former team, and protecting my Navy brothers as well as my country. That always got me fired up.

I'd brooded for months after the doc told me I wouldn't be going on any more missions. But I'd already known I couldn't. The limp in my gait would've slowed me down, and my hearing would've only gotten me killed along with others. I had the option of a desk job at some military base in the US, but working behind some desk wasn't me.

"Josh. Josh," Dad said again.

The urgency in his voice made my heart fall to my feet. I rushed to his side. "Are you okay?"

He smiled wide as he always did. The man's days were numbered, yet I could always find him smiling. He'd come to terms with his ALS. "I was dealt this card, son," he'd said many times. "Now I have to make the best of it."

I could understand his reasoning. With my hearing impairment, I had to do the same with what fate had given me. Of course my situation didn't have an end date like his.

"Can you get me my glasses?"

I snagged them off the coffee table and set them on his nose. "I need to go to the inn. Your caregiver should be here within thirty minutes. Will you be okay? Do you need to use the restroom?"

He adjusted his reading glasses. "I'll be fine. Any word from your girl?" His tone was charged with both excitement and trepidation. I knew he was worried about Liza.

"You're still trying to play matchmaker?" I teased.

"You both like each other but aren't doing anything about it. Why not? She's beautiful, your type, and I like her."

I crossed my arms. "How do you know my type?" This I had to hear. I hadn't brought any women home since high school.

He cocked one eyebrow. "Son, Riley resembles Marybeth."

I could feel a deep crease forming in between my eyes. "I don't think so." Sure, Riley and Marybeth both had black hair, but Riley's eyes were a stormy gray, and Marybeth had eyes the color of onyx.

Dad reclined in his chair. "All I'm saying is ask her out."

I tucked my hands into my jeans pockets and lowered my gaze as if I were shy talking about girls, dates, and what my dad wanted for me deep down —marriage. "I did ask her to dinner and a movie."

My dad's face glowed all of a sudden. "She said yes, I hope."

I glanced at the TV. *Good Morning, Gold Coast* was on. Dad recorded the morning show. He loved watching the mascot more than the host. Their mascot was a golden retriever named Star, who stole the show every time. Plus, Charlie seemed to notice the pretty mascot, as he barked at the screen on occasion when he was in the room. "It's hard to date a woman who doesn't live here."

"Distance doesn't matter. Woo her as much as you can while she's here. And make sure she knows how you feel, especially before she leaves. You do feel something, right?"

I harrumphed. I felt lots of things around Riley that my dad didn't need to know about. Regardless, I did want to get married someday. I wasn't opposed to dating someone steady, and Riley was the perfect candidate. Actually, she was the only one who was worming her way into my heart and my head. If I were being honest, she was setting my body on fire—a fire that would rage until our lips locked and our bodies melted together.

"I just met her. It's not like one kiss and we'll walk into the sunset and live happily ever after."

My dad gave one of those looks that said, *Right. You keep lying to yourself.* "That's what happened with your mom and me. So don't be so jaded about love."

I wasn't jaded; I was just a realist.

Star bounced onto the set, and the host, Dash Diamond, greeted her.

As if Charlie knew, he came into the room, licking his chops. When we'd gotten home from Gold Coast General, he'd beelined for his food bowl, which he hadn't touched yet that morning. He jumped up onto the sofa and got comfy as he gazed at the TV.

"I predict you two will be married within a year, two at the most," my dad said.

I full-on belly laughed, petting Charlie. "Hey, boy. Do you think I'll be married to Riley one day?"

He yawned.

On that note, I checked my phone to see if my bride-to-be had texted or left me a voice mail. *Bride-to-be.* That thought made me laugh again.

"Nothing from Riley." I kissed Dad on the head. "Charlie is staying here for a couple of hours. He looks as tired as you."

I usually gave Charlie a day or two off, although he liked to be at the inn, greeting people on occasion and staying by my side.

"We'll be napping until my caregiver gets here. Let me know if you find out anything on Liza." Worry plagued his voice.

Charlie curled up, yawning once again.

I kissed him too. "I'll be back shortly."

As soon as I was outside, I called Riley. I'd been dying to talk to her since I'd hung up with her about two hours before. I'd been checking my phone constantly too. I pressed the phone to my ear, and the line rang three times before Riley's voice mail picked up. She was probably still talking to Taylor. I didn't leave a message. I didn't want to come off as desperate, even though I was for two reasons. I was finding that her voice had a way of calming me, and I wanted news on Liza.

My next call was to Liza. Not surprisingly, her voice mail picked up the second the line connected. Then I called the SFPD to see if they had any leads on Liza since I'd filed a missing person's report.

I waited to be connected to Officer Tanner as I sauntered the one block to the inn. When I arrived at the main entrance, Tanner's voice came through the line.

"Josh, I don't have any leads. I'm sorry."

I wondered if he or anyone within his department was even trying hard. "Thanks. I also wanted to tell you that the FBI is looking for my cousin too."

"What? Since when?" Tanner asked.

"Since yesterday." When he and his partner had dragged me down to the precinct, I'd brought them up to speed on who Liza had worked for back in Boston and what I suspected.

"Honestly, maybe they'll have better luck than us. We have a high caseload."

That wasn't exactly what I wanted to hear. "Please keep trying."

I believed we had a better chance if we all worked together, or if we at least had everyone looking for Liza.

"I'll call you if I find anything," Tanner said.

Pocketing my phone, I ambled into the inn with one purpose in mind—to find Agents Wallace and Dennison.

Drake waved me over as soon as he saw me.

I circled the front desk then tapped a few keys on the computer until I found Wallace's room number.

"I take it there's no word on Liza. Did Riley get anywhere with that assistant?" Drake rubbed his bald head. "And where's Charlie?"

"No on Liza. Don't know on Riley, and Charlie is napping with my dad." I dialed Wallace's room. "Agent Wallace, Josh here. Any word from the hospitals?"

"I was just coming down to find you," Wallace said. "None of the hospitals report anyone by the name of Liza Bandon, but I do have other information. Are you free to meet me in the restaurant?"

My pulse quickened so fast, I had to catch my breath. "Can you tell me over the phone? Did you find Liza?"

"I'm on a call right now with the Boston office. We might have a breakthrough. Meet me in fifteen minutes." He sounded indifferent, giving me no hint of good news or bad.

Several expletives fell quietly from my lips as my stomach coiled. It was going to be the longest fifteen minutes of my life.

17

RILEY

Taylor picked at the nail polish on her thumb as we both sat across the mahogany desk from Mr. Gansett.

The atmosphere was ripe with tension so thick, one would've needed a chisel to break through it. Actually, a chisel sounded good right about then. Maybe I could've used the tool to knock the information out of Taylor about what else she wasn't telling me.

She fixated on her Jimmy Choo navy-blue heels. Rent might have been expensive in the city, but Taylor could've afforded a decent place other than the dump Josh and I had found her in. That much I was sure of, particularly since she was wearing a tailored blazer over a knee-length skirt that probably cost more than my plane ticket.

Mr. Gansett loosened his tie, scrutinizing Taylor and me.

Taylor fidgeted as she stole a look at her boss's boss.

His leatherback chair squeaked as he rolled it toward the desk. Then he knotted his fingers together and propped up his elbows. "Taylor, you told me Liza was on a business trip to LA this week. Is that true or not?"

I literally choked and popped up like a jack-in-the-box, ready to unleash all my anger on the thin and frail blonde—frail in the sense that she was cowering under his scrutiny.

I crossed one Capri-clad leg over the other and pierced her with a hard look.

She stuck out her angular chin. "Liza is on a business trip. At least that was what she told me. It was a last-minute change in her schedule. Ms. Norton wanted one of her designs changed. Liza had to fly to London."

I had no idea who Ms. Norton was and didn't care. "If that is true, then why can't I reach her on her phone?" I asked. "Why hasn't she called me to let me know? She wouldn't drop our plans last weekend without a phone call or an explanation. You're lying, Taylor. What are you hiding? Are you involved in Liza's disappearance? Should I have the FBI check into your background?"

She sucked in the woodsy-scented air. Mr. Gansett seemed to have bathed in a bottle of men's cologne.

She swallowed loudly. "I've done nothing wrong."

I interlocked my fingers, mostly so I wouldn't use them on her. I sighed, trying to get my nerves under control. "Look." I softened my voice. "I get the feeling you're loyal to Liza. But I also get the feeling that you know where she is."

Her jaw hardened. "How many times do I have to tell you? I don't."

I wanted to strangle her, yet I had to take a step back. No matter how hard I probed, it was clear she wasn't going to tell me anything. I looked to Mr. Gansett for help and hoped he got the silent message I was sending him with my eyes.

He cleared his throat. "Riley, tell me about the FBI and why they're looking for Liza."

I pushed a nail into my palm. I wasn't sure how much to tell him with Taylor present, although she had told the FBI about the two men looking for Liza. Then again, I didn't really know much except that Liza had called them. "I'm not sure. But I'm glad they're involved. Maybe they can find Liza."

Mr. Gansett considered Taylor.

As if his intimidating glare jolted Taylor, she said, "The FBI was here yesterday, asking to see Liza. They wanted to speak with you, but you weren't here."

He swung his gaze between Taylor and me. "Let me get this straight. Almost a week ago, Riley flew in to see Liza. But you never saw her and didn't spend the weekend with her." He lifted his eyebrows at me before he regarded Taylor. "You're now telling me that Liza is on a last-minute business trip to London to see Ms. Norton. Is that correct?"

"Yes," she said meekly.

"Taylor." Mr. Gansett's voice was deep and intimidating, reminding me of my loser father before I thought he was a worthless person. "I know you need this job. So if I find out you're lying, I will fire you on the spot." He pressed a button on his phone. "Candace, please get me Ms. Norton on the phone ASAP. Also, check with accounting to see if a plane ticket was recently booked in Liza's name to London."

Candace's light and airy voice came through the speakerphone. "Sure thing, sir."

As we waited, Mr. Gansett said, "Riley, is there anything else you can tell me about the FBI and their involvement with Liza."

Taylor, meek and scared, eyed me. She was becoming an enigma. When Josh and I had spoken to her at her apartment the other day, she seemed to have a little more courage than she did now. Sure, Mr. Gansett was on the verge of firing her if Liza wasn't meeting with Ms. Norton, and every ounce of my being knew that Liza hadn't flown to London.

I sat up straighter, shaking my head. "I can put you in touch with an Agent Wallace." It was best if Agent Wallace spoke to Mr. Gansett directly.

He smoothed two fingers over his mustache. "Does this have anything to do with her former employer?"

I suspected that Liza had been required to divulge her past employers on her resumé when she'd applied for the job at Stitches Inc. "Possibly."

The buzz of the phone trilled, causing Taylor to flinch. I'd never seen someone so nervous to the point that a sheen of sweat coated her made-up face. At any moment, her foundation would start to melt.

Mr. Gansett pressed a button on the phone.

"Patching Ms. Norton through," Candace said.

The thick tension in the room solidified into cement.

"Wayne," Ms. Norton said. "How are you?" Her voice had a rasp to it as though she were a long-time smoker.

"Delia, I'm good. I was calling to see if Liza made it to London." Mr. Gansett's hard look was riveted on Taylor.

I held my breath. If Liza had taken a plane to London, that would've explained why all my calls to her had gone straight to voice mail.

"Liza's in London?" Delia asked.

Taylor hung her head, and a tear fell on her tan skirt.

Mr. Gansett bit his lip before responding. "So she's not meeting with you about your designs?"

"No, Wayne. What's this about? Is Liza all right?"

Mr. Gansett played with his mustache. "She's fine." He didn't sound all that convincing.

I was relieved to know that I was right. Liza wasn't on a business trip. Yet I was freaked out more than ever at the notion of Liza being hurt or worse… I couldn't think about the worse. However, statistics had shown that the longer a person was missing, the more likely she wouldn't be found alive.

Tears stung my eyes. I felt as if a swarm of bees had found a home underneath my eyelids. I picked a focal point past the hefty man behind the desk and counted the number of windows on the building across the street. I'd gotten to twenty when Mr. Gansett almost shouted, "Taylor, you're fired."

I blinked once then twice, a tear escaping down my cheek.

"I swear to you that Liza told me she was headed to London to see Ms. Norton. I swear it." Her voice cracked in so many places.

As for me, I was trying to breathe.

Her nostrils flared as she swiveled her head slowly toward me. "This is all your fault."

My mouth fell to my lap, where I was digging my nails into my palms. "How so?"

She mashed her lips into a thin line. "I needed this job."

I couldn't help but laugh.

"Taylor, I need you to clean out your desk," Mr. Gansett said as though he were used to firing people, which he probably was, given that he was the boss.

Courage seeped into Taylor's eyes and washed over her body as she wagged her finger at me. Meek Taylor was gone, and a demon of sorts bloomed to life. "You will pay for this"

Mr. Gansett became a water stain on the window as I narrowed my focus to Taylor. "Tell me what you know about Liza." I said rather than asked.

Taylor's blue eyes were telling me nothing but showed her defiance. She was standing her ground. Maybe she wasn't lying after all. But one thing bothered me.

"Who were you talking to when I found you in Liza's office?"

"You wouldn't believe me if I told you," she said calmly. Then she rose, tugging down her tan blazer. "I'll pack my things." She started for the door.

"Taylor," Mr. Gansett said. "It might help your situation if you answer Riley's question."

Slowly, she turned, her arms hanging at her sides. "I doubt it. But if you must know, I was talking to Liza." Then she left without another word.

I didn't have time to gasp before my phone rang in my purse. I was certain it was Josh checking on me. But my body seemed glued to the chair.

I couldn't say how long I sat dumbfounded, but the ringing of my phone once again zapped the life back into me.

I grabbed my bag and bolted out the door. I had to find Taylor.

Mr. Gansett called my name, but I kept going. Taylor was the only person I wanted to talk to.

The hallway was empty. I ran to every office on the floor. No Taylor. I checked the restroom. No Taylor.

I asked Candace where Taylor went.

"She ran out and into the elevator," Candace said. "What's going on?"

I wished I knew.

My phone would stop ringing then start up again. I took the elevator down to the lobby, but I struck out in finding Taylor.

I had to give her props for her disappearing act.

I hurried outside and into a cluster of people going in all directions, when my darn phone went off again.

"What?" I answered in a rude tone. Then I held my breath. If it were a client, I would be mortified.

"Oh my God. Finally."

"Liza, is that you?"

The world around me came to a complete stop.

18

———

JOSH

The restaurant at the inn was teeming with guests sitting down for lunch. Tables were filling up fast, and Agent Wallace hadn't come down from his room. My diver's watch indicated he had two minutes. If he wasn't on time, I would go to him. One of my flaws was impatience, which had gotten me into trouble a time or two. In fact, it had almost gotten an American killed.

Our team had been surveilling a known enemy of the US in the mountains of Afghanistan. Our job had been to gather data—who went in, who came out, and any activity that would help us find two reporters who had been captured. Our commander had told us not to engage under any circumstances.

But the gun to the reporter's head had spurred me into action, and my instinct had been to save him. Hell, it was a normal human reaction. Luckily, one of my teammates caught me before I'd ruined the mission, and even though we'd been successful in saving the two Americans, I had gotten my butt chewed out, and I'd deserved it.

Right now, though, I wasn't spying on a known terrorist. I didn't have to worry about others getting killed. I just needed answers. Time was ticking away, and the more days that passed, the more my hope of finding Liza dwindled.

The elevator dinged, and Wallace sauntered out as if he didn't have a care in the world. He'd ditched the suit from yesterday and donned a pair of black slacks and a white golf shirt with the FBI emblem embroidered in the upper left. I expected to see a gun at his hip or a holster around him, but he came across like a man ready to play golf.

I dipped my head in the opposite direction of the restaurant. "Let's use my office. I need the space quiet so I can hear you." We didn't need anyone eavesdropping either.

When we were seated inside, he asked, "How did you lose your hearing?"

The man wanted to chitchat, when all I wanted to do was tell him to cut the bull.

"I see from your tat that you were a SEAL? A mission gone wrong?"

I briefly glanced at my tat, which read, "The Only Easy Day Was Yesterday." That was the truth. No one understood the meaning more than SEALs. Regardless, I decided to humor Wallace to give myself a chance to quiet my nerves. Otherwise, the meeting wouldn't go well. Or worse, it could land me in jail for assaulting a federal agent.

"I was in an explosion on a classified mission. I hate to be rude, but what's the breakthrough you mentioned?" I picked up a pen that was lying right where I'd left it after signing employee checks.

He grinned as though he was proud of me for getting straight to the point. "Where's Riley? We need her to look at some photos of the men in the SUV."

"Shouldn't you be showing them to Taylor?" She'd gotten the best look at the men.

"We will." He gave me his phone. "Is that the SUV you saw at Liza's apartment?"

I studied the photo. I could see two men through the windshield, which wasn't tinted. The driver had dark hair as Riley had mentioned, but the passenger was the man Taylor had described— bald head and goatee. He also had tanned skin; dark, beady eyes; and a piercing in his left ear.

If I weren't mistaken, Baldy was glancing out the driver's side window, giving me the impression that he saw Riley.

My blood gelled. If he'd seen her, then she could be in danger too. "Do you know who these men are?"

He crossed one leg over the other. "Riley might be right about Moretti's men showing up in California. We pulled a video from the cameras on the street that Liza lives on. The bald guy we believe works for Moretti. The driver is none other than Moretti's son."

My muscles tensed. "Seems to me they've pegged Riley. She could be in danger."

"Where is she?"

"She went into the city to talk to Taylor. She still believes Taylor is hiding something."

Wallace collected his phone. "That may be, but all we could drum up on Taylor was she's a rich girl from a rich family, with daddy issues."

That explained her expensive clothes, and daddy issues might've explained why she was living in a rundown building. Maybe Rich Girl was trying to show her father that she could cut it on her own.

"Dennison and I are headed out to meet two agents from the SF FBI office at Liza's place. Then we'll stop by and show these photos to Taylor. In the meantime, my team is working on getting a better angle of the SUV and the license plate. I'll text you the photo."

"I want to go with you." I knew he wouldn't allow that, but I asked nonetheless. My dad had always taught me that it never hurt to ask. All a person could do was say no. "I know Liza's neighbor. He might open up more if I'm there." *Part lie. Part truth.*

He leaned forward. "The best thing for you to do is stay put. My team and I got this." He rubbed his thumb over his forefinger. "You miss the hunt, the adrenaline rush of missions. Don't you?"

I hitched a shoulder. "I'll never be a SEAL again."

"No, but have you thought about law enforcement?"

I let out a laugh as I pointed to my left ear. "Completely deaf in this ear." Then I touched my right. "I can barely hear out of this one. What makes you think I could protect my partner's back if I was a cop or an agent?" I was digging the idea until I thought of my dad.

"Josh." Wallace used a fatherly tone, as if I were his son. I could've been, given his age. "The DEA is always recruiting. You could be a dog handler. Where is your service dog by the way?"

I stood, extending my hand. "Home with my dad. Thank you for the advice, and as much as I would love the idea, I couldn't entertain anything like that since my dad's health prevents me from doing anything other than managing the inn."

We exchanged a handshake.

"I'll give you a call later this evening," Wallace said. "Dennison and I will be staying in the city."

"Let me see where Riley is. She might be on her way back." I tapped on her number in my phone then hit the speaker button. The line went directly to voice mail.

Surely, she should be finished with Taylor by now. It was well after noon. Granted, the drive there and back would take hours, let alone the fact that two women could talk for a long time.

He padded to the door. "If Riley does get anything of value from Taylor, please call me." Then he waltzed out.

I rubbed my jaw, deciding what to do next. His breakthrough was weak at best. He was no further on finding Liza than the SFPD.

My phone rang, and Riley's name came across the screen.

"Are you okay?" I answered. "Where are you? Did you get any info from Taylor?" I couldn't contain myself. My breathing sped up.

"Josh, Liza just called me."

"What! Where is she?"

"I don't know. I lost the connection. She sounded rushed and frightened."

"Where are you?"

"I'm at a coffee shop one block down from the Stitches office building. I've been hoping she would call me back."

"Redial the number. Did she call you from her phone?"

"That's the problem. The call came in with no caller ID."

"Stay put. I'm on my way. Text me the name of the coffee shop."

"We should tell the agents." Her voice cracked a little.

"Not much to tell them if you don't know anything, and you don't have a number they can trace."

She expelled a heavy sigh.

"Riley, I want you to watch over your shoulder. Wallace found out that the dark-haired man you saw in the SUV is none other than Moretti's son. The verdict is still out on the bald guy."

Her tone rose in pitch. "For real?"

"Baby doll, don't move from that coffee shop. I'll be there as soon as I can."

She whimpered. "I like it when you call me baby doll."

Man, if she whimpered one more time, I might have to take a cold shower.

19

RILEY

With shaky fingers, I texted Josh as soon as we hung up, although when he'd called me baby doll, I'd melted into a puddle of mush where I sat.

The Coffee Bean Factory was busy with patrons coming and going for their afternoon caffeine fix. Many were absorbed in their phones or talking to their friends. I would've given anything to talk to Liza again. One moment, she had been there, and the next, she'd been gone.

I sat at a table near the window with my phone in front of me, willing Liza to call again. I bit on a chipped nail. I'd gotten a manicure before I'd left Boston, but I had been chewing away on my nails, which was so unlike me.

I shifted my attention out the window. The streets were jammed with cars stopped at the red light. Business people—big, small, tall, short, dressed in jackets with scarves around their necks—hurried in all directions. Some waited for the signal to cross the street.

The sun's rays sprayed down in between the dense cluster of buildings in the financial district.

Where are you, Liza? What in the world is going on?

Tears stung my eyes as anger gripped my stomach. Liza was

alive. I should've been relieved, but I wasn't. I was confused and ready to scream at my best friend. She'd let me and her family believe she could be hurt.

Josh pinged me with a text. *I'm stuck in traffic.*

No surprise there.

I sighed at the thought of Josh. A man I hardly knew who had all the qualities of a perfect boyfriend, husband, and soulmate was seeping into my heart little by little. Aside from how attracted I was to him or how much he occupied my mind, I was grateful he was helping me. Sure, he was Liza's family, but he had a major priority in taking care of his dad and running a business.

I replied. *Liza hasn't called again.*

Are you sure it was her?

I didn't have to think about that question. I knew Liza's voice, especially when she dropped the line, "Oh my God." She always punctuated each word in a dramatic fashion. I'd always teased her about how expressive she was. Her response had been, "I'm a valley girl through and through."

I smiled at that. I missed my friend. We were supposed to have had fun the past week. Yet the only good thing that had happened since I'd landed in the Golden State was meeting Josh.

Riley, are you there?

Yes. I'm sure it was Liza. How long do you think you'll be?

I couldn't sit around much longer. If Taylor had spoken to Liza, then she might know where Liza was.

I typed a response to Josh. *I'm going to find Taylor and make her talk.*

No. Wait for me.

I would seriously wait for him forever if Liza weren't in trouble.

My phone danced on the metal table, displaying the words "No caller ID." *Liza.*

I snatched up the phone. "Where are you?" My voice was hard and high.

"Sorry," Liza said, out of breath. "I thought Moretti's men had found us."

"Us?" I'd suspected Moretti's men were in town, so that wasn't a surprise.

"Haley and I are in hiding."

"Hurry up," I heard a mousy voice say in the background.

"Where are you? Hell, woman, Josh and I have been worried sick. So has Drake and Josh's dad. What is going on?" My voice ticked higher and higher on each word.

"I can't talk. I need your help."

I let out a nervous laugh. "Now? Why not a week ago?"

Maybe we weren't as close as I thought we were.

"Riley," Liza said my name in warning. "I don't have time to explain. Please." She lost the hard edge to her voice on the last word.

As much as I wanted answers, her plea broke my heart, tempering my anger for the moment. "I'm listening."

"I was talking to Taylor when she hung up on me. Now I can't get a hold of her. Can you track her down? Have her go into my office and look for a green thumb drive."

I massaged one side of my head. I could feel a headache blooming.

"Riley." Liza sounded irritated. "Are you still there?

Maybe in body, but not mind. Liza was going to croak when I told her Taylor got fired. "Um. Mr. Gansett fired Taylor."

"What?" Her voice hitched. "How do you know that?"

"Long story."

"Liza," the mousy voice said. "Hurry up. They're probably tracking the call."

"One minute, Haley," Liza barked at her. "If we don't get that drive, we're both dead."

"We're dead anyway," Haley snapped.

Hearing the word "dead" made me feel as if a thousand needles were poking me all at once.

I swallowed thickly. "What can I do?"

"Can you go to my office? There's a short filing cabinet next to the window. The green thumb drive is taped to the underside of the top drawer."

"Sure. I'm at The Coffee Bean Factory a block from your building. I just need to figure out how to get past the piranha, Candace, your receptionist." I might have to barter with the woman again, which was totally fine. Maybe I should just plan her wedding free of charge. I could use that as an excuse to return to California. After all, Liza owed me a tour of her home state, and I wouldn't mind seeing Josh again.

"Figure something out. Better yet, find Taylor. She'll help you."

I shook my head, even though Liza couldn't see me. "She won't. Trust me."

"Riley, Taylor will."

Maybe she would if I could find her. "What do I do when I get the thumb drive?"

"I'm working on that," she said. "I got to run. I'll call you tonight. Take Josh with you for protection."

A flirty and nervous laugh escaped me. "Speaking of Josh, why haven't you called him?" He had courage, strength, probably weapons, a take-no-prisoners attitude, and he was an ex-Navy SEAL.

"You've met my cousin, right? He's ready to strap on a gun and all his SEAL gear and fight again. We don't need mafia men all over Redwood Cove."

Met him, kissed him, held his hand, flirted with him, slept in his house, and will probably cry when I have to leave him.

The small, sleepy resort town didn't need men with guns storming the streets, and neither did the inn. The agents had shown up, but they were the good guys. *Speaking of the FBI…*

"Liza, one more thing."

Silence filled the line.

"Liza." I glanced at my phone, and the screen showed all my apps instead of a connected call. *Well, crap on a cracker.*

Sighing, I sat for a minute, debating whether I should wait for Josh. He might be able to use his handsomeness and gentlemanly charm on Candace.

Time was of the essence, though, and Josh was stuck in traffic. He could've been a good hour or more away. Besides, I could get the drive and be back at the coffee shop before Josh even got into the city.

Fifteen minutes later, I was walking back into Stitches Inc. The reception desk was empty, and the fifteenth floor was quiet, too quiet. Biting my nail, I debated whether to wait for someone before I went snooping around. The last thing I wanted to do was get thrown out before I retrieved the thumb drive.

I steeled my nerves, rushed into Liza's office, and closed the door with gentle ease. I swallowed my nerves, then found the short filing cabinet that Liza had spoken of. I stuck my hand in and felt around on the underside of the top, but the wood was smooth with no signs of a thumb drive. Maybe I hadn't heard her right. I turned, and when I did, I squealed and slapped a hand over my heart.

"Looking for something?" Mr. Gansett asked in a not-so-nice voice.

What the heck happened to the nice guy I met earlier?

I tried to speak, but words failed me.

He tucked his hands into his pants pockets. "I've been through this office, and you won't find what Liza is looking for." His tone was devoid of any emotion.

"Let me guess. You have the thumb drive."

"Actually, I don't. But you're going to lead me to it."

Immediately, Taylor came to mind. She had to have it.

He whipped out his phone. "Get up here."

My pulse started to gallop. All I could think about were Haley's words. *"We're dead anyway."*

I didn't want to die, but I also wouldn't go down without a fight. The problem was I had no way out except past Mr. Gansett. He was a large man and could probably stop me in a flash.

As I thought of my next move, I couldn't help but remember something my mom had warned me about. "Sweetie, men can strap on the charm, but underneath all that chivalry can be a snake waiting to bite."

Mr. Gansett was a snake and a great actor. He'd given me no indication he was in bed with the mafia.

I tossed a look over my shoulder for nothing more than to give myself a minute to think of an escape route. But jumping through a window fifteen stories up wasn't an option.

My body stiffened when I saw two large men in the reflection of the window. My blood froze solid. I turned ever so slowly, trying not to panic, but that was futile.

One of the men had biceps the size of Mount Everest. The other had a muscular build, but what rendered me speechless was his bald head. He was the same dude I'd seen in the black SUV.

Mr. Gansett waved them in. "Take her and get me her phone."

I should've been shaking in my flats. I should've been screaming bloody murder. But Ross had always taught me to stay calm if I were ever cornered.

"The more you fight, the more you run the risk of getting hurt, or even worse —killed," he'd said. *"Wait for the right moment to attack when they're not expecting it."*

Mr. Gansett whispered to both men.

That one or two seconds gave me ample time to get my phone out of my purse. As I dug around inside, I was failing at the only task that could probably save my life. I had to call Josh or at least send him a text.

I continued to feel around in my bag, not taking my eyes off the men.

Mount Everest Man studied me for a beat before he stalked over, holding out his hand. "Give me your purse."

My breathing ramped up as I backed away the closer he got. Before I could take my next breath, I was up against the window.

His large paw came at me. I ducked and ran toward the door.

Baldy blocked me with an evil smirk on his pocked face.

Mr. Gansett crossed his arms over his chest. The pinhead was enjoying all this.

I inched backward, right into the arms of Mount Everest, who threw my purse on the desk. The sound exploded in the room, causing me to jerk, and when I did, Mount Everest let go of me.

"You won't be needing this," Mount Everest said as he tossed my phone to Mr. Gansett.

Suddenly, I wanted to cry. I had no way out and no way to call for help. Staying calm was out of the question.

Mount Everest wrapped his fingers around my arms and squeezed as though he was trying to juice a lemon.

Anger, hot and maddening, made me bite down on my tongue as tears stung. I wasn't going down without a fight. I swung my body around as best I could and kneed Mount Everest in the crotch, another thing Ross had taught me. *"Always go for a guy's manhood."* Well, he hadn't said it so eloquently.

Mount Everest bent over, grunting and wincing.

"She's a fighter," Mr. Gansett said with a smile in his voice.

I darted around Everest and circled the desk, breathing so darn heavy, I thought my lungs would collapse. I looked for anything that could be used as a weapon, while Baldy and Mr. Gansett just stood there.

They knew I wasn't getting past them. They also knew I had no chance of hurting them. I didn't care. The longer I kept them in the office, trying to get free, the more chance I had of someone in the building showing up. I hoped someone who worked there would peek in to see what all the commotion was about. That was one time I wanted Candace to catch me in the act.

"Bart," Mr. Gansett said. "Get her out of here now. Use the back entrance."

Baldy grinned, seemingly enjoying the chase.

I grabbed the closest thing to me—a stapler. "Baldy Bart." I giggled like a school kid who had just heard the funniest thing. The name Baldy Bart seemed funny as nerves overtook my entire being.

Then in a blur, Bart covered my nose with a piece of white fabric, and the room around me went dark.

20

JOSH

I growled, itching to throw my phone out the window. Riley wasn't answering. It seemed that no matter who I called lately, no one picked up anymore. But with traffic moving, I couldn't text her.

Charlie perked up his head as we went over the bridge into the city. "As soon as we get to the coffee shop," I said to Charlie, "I'm going to kiss Riley like she's never been kissed before. Then we'll check in with Agent Wallace." Aside from those two things, I had no other plan.

I tried Riley again.

When I got her voice mail, my gut plummeted to the floorboard as I braked at a red light. It was the same feeling I'd gotten that day I went into the apartment building in Afghanistan. My stomach got tight. My body shivered. That always happened right before something big went down.

I puffed out my cheeks, saying a silent prayer as the light turned green. After two more blocks, I found a parking garage. Within five minutes, Charlie and I were walking into the Coffee Bean Factory not far from Stitches Inc.

I walked around but didn't have to. The comfy coffee shop was small enough to see everyone and everything right from the entrance. Patrons lounged in living-room-style chairs, at tables, and a few at the high bar that surrounded the barista area.

Not one black-haired woman who made my mouth dry and my body sizzle with heat sat among the crowd. Nevertheless, I asked the short young girl making the coffee if she'd seen a woman of average height with long black hair that probably appeared dark blue in the light, gray eyes, and snow-white skin. I'd forgotten what Riley was wearing.

"Sir, you know you just described most of the ladies that walk in here," the girl said.

My pulse ramped up.

Charlie pulled on his leash.

I glanced down and let him lead me. He sniffed his way over to a table by the window, where a middle-aged hippie sat absorbed in his laptop.

Charlie continued to sniff around his table and the empty one in front of him.

"Excuse me," I said to the hippie, who was wearing his hair up in a man bun. I wouldn't have been caught dead with that hairstyle, not because I was a Navy SEAL and the buzz cut was uniform issue, but long hair on men wasn't my thing.

He eyed me, dragging dirty nails down his unshaven face. The only time I didn't shave was when we were deep in the mountains of Afghanistan and shaving was the last thing any of us had on our hygiene list.

Charlie nuzzled the chair as if to tell me Riley had been sitting there.

"Have you been here long? I'm looking for a lady, pretty, long black hair, gray eyes—"

"She smells like cherries?" he asked.

My jaw came unhinged. "Yeah." I thought I was the only one who'd noticed that.

The hippie held out his hand to Charlie. "I overheard her talking to someone named Liza. Then she took off and went that way." He pointed a finger in the direction of Stitches Inc.

"How long ago? Did you hear anything else? Like where she could be going?"

"Um, she left about an hour ago. And other than the name Liza, I heard her say Taylor."

"Thanks, man." I hightailed it out and started toward Stitches Inc. Riley had mentioned in one of her texts that she was going to make Taylor talk.

Charlie and I waltzed into the fashion company ten minutes later and were greeted with no one. I checked my watch to see if the workday had ended, but it was approaching four p.m.

"Hello," I called out, glancing down both hallways.

Charlie and I started with the offices on the opposite end from where Liza's was located. With each door we opened, we found a room that was barebones empty. Then we started looking in the offices on Liza's end.

I felt as if I were in a *Walking Dead* episode in which Rick used caution when he scoured a building. I'd had to do just that in many missions, but missions and normal life in a big city were by far on the opposite ends of the spectrum.

Charlie managed to tug his way out of my grasp and slipped into an office two doors down from Liza's.

"Charlie?" I called in more of a whisper.

Charlie came out of the office and nudged my hand with his wet nose. Then he darted back inside. His actions told me he'd heard a noise that he wanted me to know about.

A large cherry-stained desk, a credenza with liquor on display, and a wall full of photos of models and photographers decorated the plush room.

Charlie trotted to the closet then sat on his haunches.

"Is someone in there?"

I wasn't on a mission, so I shouldn't have been apprehensive. I studied Charlie as I closed my hand around the knob, praying a bomb wouldn't go off. I knew I was overreacting, but that fateful day would always be fresh in my mind.

Slowly, I opened the door and gasped.

Red, or Candace, if I remembered her name, was tied and

gagged as tears streamed down her face, cutting a path through her makeup.

I made quick work of untying her.

When she was free, she threw her arms around me, practically tackling me to the ground. "I'm so glad you didn't obey the rules."

I knew she was referring to the fact that I hadn't listened to her the last time I'd been there.

I peeled her off me, needing answers. "What's going on? And please speak loudly. I'm deaf in my left ear."

She fixed her hair, which was wild and free, then flicked her fingers over her eyes and cheeks. "You wouldn't believe me if I told you." She shuddered.

Try me came to mind, but instead, I said, "I'm looking for Riley. Have you seen her? Or Liza? Has Liza shown up? And where is everyone? This place is like a ghost town."

She scratched Charlie's ears, muttering something I couldn't make out because I couldn't see her lips.

I tapped her on the shoulder. Normally, I wouldn't mind anyone giving Charlie some love, but we were wasting time.

"Sorry," she practically shouted. "Mr. Gansett and his men took Riley."

I swayed on my feet, swearing like a sailor that I would seriously kill anyone who dared to touch Riley. "Come again. You mean Liza's boss?" I'd never met the man, but Liza had spoken his name a time or two and had nothing but good things to say about him.

Candace sat down in one of the wooden armchairs. "Yes."

"Tell me everything up to the point of how you ended up in the closet."

"I was just coming out of the bathroom when I heard Riley's voice in Liza's office. I was about to find out why she returned, but Mr. Gansett started talking. He didn't sound like the nice man I knew. At first, I thought good for him for finally putting his foot down about Riley just walking in like she worked here. But then he said, 'I've been through this office, and you won't find what Liza is looking for.' That made me pause. So I listened. Riley and Mr. Gansett went back and forth about a thumb drive. Finally, Mr.

Gansett told Riley that she was going to help him get the thumb drive."

Liza must've had it, which was why her place had been ransacked.

Charlie lay down at my feet. "How did you end up in the closet?"

She wiped the area underneath her eyes. "I heard the elevator ding. So I ducked back into the bathroom then came out as if I'd heard nothing. I was walking back to reception, when two big men, one bald with a goatee and the other with thick black hair and easy on the eyes, stalked down the hall. I smiled and proceeded to sit at my desk. I didn't know what to do, but I had to somehow help Riley." She inhaled and blew out a breath. "I couldn't hear from where I sat. So I got as close to Liza's office as I could. Mr. Gansett told the men to take Riley and her phone. Then Mr. Gansett said to the men that Taylor probably has the thumb drive. Before I could move, Mr. Gansett came out of the office and caught me."

I shoved my hand through my hair and pulled. I needed to feel pain.

Take a breath, man. Riley is a tough woman. Tough or not, I had to save her. That was who I was. I saved people. I'd done it many times on SEAL missions. *But you had Intel on where those prisoners were. You had a team of SEALs backing you up. You had tactical gear. And most of all, you were one hundred percent healthy. Besides, you don't know where to look. You can't hear well enough to walk into a sticky situation, let alone run with your bad leg.*

I growled low, and Charlie perked up.

Candace regarded me with tears streaming down her face. "We need to find Riley. We need to call the cops. We need to call Taylor." She wiped her eyes. "What is Liza into?"

The same question I had.

I waved a hand around. "The entire floor is empty. Am I missing something?"

She swiped a hand under her nose. "Several of the offices on this floor have never been occupied as long as I've worked here.

Plus, three of the managers are away on business. Josh, thank you. If you hadn't found me, then I might have died in that closet."

I doubted she would've died. "Do you know where Taylor is or where she could be? Anything?"

"Taylor was fired." Then her eyes went wide. "I think Mr. Gansett has Riley's phone. You could try calling it."

"I have."

Now it was time to call in the cavalry.

21

RILEY

The scent of something pungent and disgusting made me choke. But the odor wasn't as bad as the pain in my head. It felt as if someone had whacked me several times with a sledgehammer.

As a male voice drilled through my fuzziness, I found myself on the floor of a van, surrounded by musty blankets that stank of urine. I sat up, or tried to, when my head banged against the side metal wall of the van.

"She's awake," a male voice said.

I knew that voice. It was the same person I'd kneed in the crotch. In record speed, my mind cleared.

Pressing my hands to the floor, I managed to push to a sitting position then oriented my vision to find that we were parked in some alley. At least I assumed we were from the dumpster behind the rotund man standing outside the van's door.

I blinked, and Mr. Gansett came into focus. He'd shucked his business suit for a pair of jeans that looked odd on the hefty man. I desperately wanted to call the fashion police. A laugh bubbled to the surface. He owned a fashion company, and I wanted to tell him that high-waisted jeans were out of style. At least I thought they were. In fact, Josh wore his jeans low on his hips.

Oh my. Josh. My muscles tightened. He was probably worried sick that I wasn't at the coffee shop. I took inventory of my body. My hands were tied behind my back, my mouth was gagged with the same fabric Baldy or Bart had shoved over my nose, and my ankles were wrapped in thick rope like the kind used to secure a boat to a pier. Nevertheless, I wiggled, kicked, and screamed, but no one would hear me since my mouth was gagged.

Mr. Gansett was wearing a smirk that I wanted to rip off.

"Where are we?" I tried to ask, scanning every nook and crevice in the beat-up van.

The only window that existed was the windshield, which I couldn't see through since Mount Everest was blocking my view. It wouldn't have mattered anyway to know where I was since Mr. Gansett had my phone.

Mount Everest waved.

Really? "How's the crotch?" I was talking to myself since my words were garbled.

Mr. Gansett glanced toward the back of the van. "Well."

Bart appeared, his bald head shiny or maybe oily. "Taylor isn't there. And the Feds are all over Liza's apartment. They won't find the thumb drive. Moretti and I tore that place apart." Bart stabbed a finger at Mount Everest.

I whipped my head toward Mount Everest. So he was a Moretti? He wasn't the one that the FBI wanted to put in prison. I'd seen pictures of the old man in the media. Mount Everest was far from old, although now that I was really looking at him, I could see that he resembled the elder Moretti with his dark hair and dark eyes.

Moretti grinned, showing pearly whites. "Yeah, you're right. I'm Stefano Moretti's son, Leo."

I must've had that question written all over my face.

"Get in," Mr. Gansett said to Bart. "It's time for our next move."

I tugged at the rope around my wrists, hoping to break free, although for the moment, I was safe. After all, they needed me to accomplish their goal.

Mr. Gansett climbed in, and the van moved with the weight of his body. He sat on a crate opposite me then pulled out my phone from the back of his jeans pocket. "What's your passcode?"

I rolled my eyes, hoping he would get the message that he was a moron. Then again, he didn't strike me as the mafia type. So maybe he hadn't kidnapped anyone before.

"Take off the gag," Bart said. "No one is going to hear her. We're in an alley."

Mr. Gansett hesitated then acquiesced.

I coughed then spit on the floor, taking in a few deep breaths. "Idiot."

Leo chuckled. "I like her, even though she probably ruined my chances of having kids."

Again, I rolled my eyes. "Seriously, Mount Everest?"

Leo's eyebrows came together, as did Bart's.

"Never mind. I'm sure you'll still have kids." Before I could utter another word, my phone rang.

In a blur, the phone was in Mr. Gansett's fat hands. "It seems Liza's cousin Josh is in a panic over your disappearance."

"He's an ex-Navy SEAL," Bart said. I detected envy in his voice.

The phone continued to trill in the small space, and my heart proceeded to beat wildly. If my hands and ankles weren't tied, I would've tackled the fat man.

Mr. Gansett chewed on his lip. "From what Liza has told me, he's been injured in combat. He's worthless. Besides, he can't do anything over the phone."

Growling, I used all the energy I could to kick the crate he was sitting on. The nice thing about gravity was that the heavier something was, the harder it fell. Gansett listed to one side, then his butt hit the floor.

I giggled. He didn't.

My phone slid under a blanket. The ringing stopped. So did my pulse, mainly because Mr. Gansett was primed to backhand me.

I stuck out my chin, ready to take whatever he was about to dish out. I would take the pain because in the end, I'd enjoyed seeing him fall. I also believed in karma. He would get what was coming to him. I just prayed it was before he killed me.

The ringing started up again.

While Mr. Gansett got back on the crate, Bart collected my phone, sneering at me in the process. "Hello."

Silence rained down as Leo, Mr. Gansett, and I watched Bart's expression morph into surprise.

Maybe Josh could be scary over the phone. Or maybe Agent Wallace was on the line.

Bart put the phone on speaker.

"Where is she?" Liza asked in a voice I didn't recognize.

I sighed. "I'm right here."

Scooting to the edge of his seat, Leo leaned in near the phone. "Love bug."

Love bug? I snorted.

Bart shook his head as if disgusted. Mr. Gansett's expression was blank.

"Leo," Liza said. "How are you?"

"Aside from me missing you, my old man is deeply hurt that you would screw him."

Liza tsked. "You know I kept my mouth shut when the FBI raided his office building. I've told you that every single time you've called me since I moved out here."

We were all riveted to the conversation as if we were listening to a good radio show.

Leo frowned, reminding me of a sad puppy. "Until now. Love bug, I need that thumb drive. I don't want to hurt you."

"You can't hurt me anymore than you have," Liza said in a tone I couldn't quite decipher.

It was official. I didn't know my best friend. She'd never shared anything with me about Leo. I guessed I could see the attraction. He was handsome, in great physical shape, and could probably smile the panties off any woman except me. I wasn't into big, beefy men. I didn't know Liza was either.

"I don't have it," she replied. "Riley, are you okay?"

"I'm fine," I shouted. I was surprised and tired, plus I missed home, my brother, and my mom. Above all else, I wanted to see Josh again.

"Riley, oh my God. How in the world did they capture you?"

I laughed. "Mr. Gansett, do you want to tell her?"

"Wayne?" Shock rocked Liza's tone. "You work for Moretti?"

"Love bug, your boss is my uncle," Leo said. "His wife and my mom are sisters."

"Family comes first, Liza," Mr. Gansett announced proudly.

That was one thing I couldn't disagree with.

Holy moly. Liza had the deck stacked against her when it came to jobs.

"I hate to break up this love fest," Bart said. "The thumb drive, Liza."

"I told you I don't have it," Liza said.

Mr. Gansett rubbed two fingers over his bushy mustache. "But Taylor does. Call Taylor. Tell her to meet me at Stitches in one hour with the thumb drive." He set his brown eyes on me. "Once we get it, we'll let Riley go."

As crazy as it might sound, I believed him. He didn't strike me as a man who would kill anyone.

Bart chewed on his lip. "Liza, you know how we operate. You know that Mr. Moretti always gets what he wants."

"I also know that I'm not stupid. So listen up." I'd never heard her so confident and brave before. "We do this on my terms. I know that the thumb drive has incriminating information that lists all Moretti's business dealings. That could not only put him away for a long time, but also his clients like the Mexican cartel. So the only way you're getting that thumb drive is if you let Haley, Riley, and Taylor walk away unharmed."

"Are you saying that you're going to bring me the thumb drive personally?" Leo could barely contain his excitement.

Bart growled. "Your old man is going to kill you if you screw this up."

Leo threw him the middle finger.

"Oh, and Liza," Bart said. "No cops or feds. If we get wind of them, then you'll never see your friend again."

On that note, a cold chill blanketed me. If anyone in the van meant what he said, it was Bart.

"If we're throwing out threats, then hear mine," Liza said. "I'll meet you at Stitches in two hours. In return, you'll let Riley go unharmed. If, however, anything happens to Riley in the meantime, then I will go public to the major TV outlets with all the data on that drive."

Leo didn't seem phased by Liza's threat. However, Bart and Mr. Gansett had their mouths slightly open.

I wasn't sure, but publicizing incriminating information had to be worse than the FBI getting ahold of it.

I was beginning to seriously think that Leo knew the plan. Or Leo was so in love with my friend that he would do anything for her.

Bart regarded Mr. Gansett, then said to Liza, "Two hours."

Let the fun begin.

22

JOSH

I paced the empty hall of Stitches Inc., calling Riley repeatedly. I was at the point where I wanted to throw the phone in the trash. Charlie stood idly by outside the men's room, watching me. He always knew when something was bothering me. The dog was ready to rescue me at a moment's notice.

I tried Agent Wallace several times to no avail. Candace tried Taylor but also got no answer. We were striking out big time. Maybe she'd been kidnapped too.

Candace emerged from the ladies' room. Her bright-red hair was tamed, and her blue eyes were clearer. "Any luck on the FBI guy yet?" she shouted.

I groaned, wanting to pull each strand of my hair out of my head. "No."

She stuck her hands on her hips. Irritation supplanted the fear she'd had earlier. "Then call that officer you know at the SFPD. I'm really worried about Riley. I'm going to try Taylor again."

I would've thought that Candace would've left by then to run for her life. But the woman was adamant about helping.

"You should go home," I said. "I'll give Agent Wallace your info. He can question you later."

She lowered her shoulders. "I told you I'm not leaving. I know if I were in Riley or Taylor's situation, I would want anyone and everyone helping to find me. Plus, I really like Riley."

I could feel a grin forming. I really liked Riley too. Suddenly, my lips tingled as if she were kissing me again.

Snap out of it, dude. Find her, then reminisce. Or better yet, take control and kiss her lights out.

"You're smitten with Riley, aren't you?" Her smile brightened in the dimly lit hall. Then she got a faraway look in her eyes as though she were thinking of her significant other.

It was my turn to break her out of her reverie, so I cupped her elbow.

"Sorry," she said. "I'll call Taylor. You call that officer at the SFPD." Her tone was commanding, as if she were leading a platoon.

As she disappeared into Liza's office, I pinched the bridge of my nose. Officer Tanner couldn't do anything to help me. Or maybe he could. But first, I decided to try Wallace again.

"Wallace," he rushed out.

Finally. I wanted to jump through the phone and give him a manly hug. "It's Josh Bandon. We have a problem. Riley was kidnapped by that bald guy in your photo."

"You know this how?" His tone was reserved, unlike mine.

"One of Liza's coworkers. It seems the mafia is looking for a thumb drive."

"Tell me where you are," Wallace demanded.

Charlie took off down the hall.

I froze.

Then he banked around to the elevators.

"Um, let me call you back." I hung up as my stomach flipped all over the place.

I stalked down the hall as fast as I could, sticking close to the wall. Before I could stop it, memories of that day came barreling back. It was always the same memory on repeat, like a broken record. Sometimes the entire memory replayed, and other times, only parts.

As I limped my way along the wall, dark eyes flashed before me.

He studied me as though I was the weirdest person he'd ever seen. Then he blessed himself before he pressed the detonator he was holding.

Less than a second was all I had to pray for my life.

My chest rose and fell, my breathing labored.

"Josh."

The woman's voice sounded like an extremely loud angel.

Something wet tickled my hand.

A light tap to my face drew me out of my trance, and I blinked several times.

A woman with wide blue eyes examined me as if she were my doctor. My gaze roamed all over her. Her hair was blond, much like the nurse who had taken care of me in the hospital.

After an intake of breath, the bright lights of the reception area came into view, along with a familiar face. "Taylor?"

She smiled. "There you are."

Candace's nose was wrinkled. "What's wrong with him?"

Charlie licked my hand.

I patted his head. "I'm fine, boy." I wasn't in the least. I was useless. I couldn't save Riley or Liza if my life depended on it.

"You wigged out." Taylor flicked a hair from my forehead. "And you're sweating. Maybe you should sit down."

I knew that day would haunt me for the rest of my life, but man, I couldn't be tapping out in the middle of trying to rescue my girlfriend and cousin. *Wait. Girlfriend?* I rolled that word around on my tongue a few times. Riley would make a great girlfriend. But titles and statuses of what we were would have to wait, although I knew the minute I found her would be the minute I dropped to my knees and asked her to marry me. *I can't be thinking of marriage. I only just met her.* Still, she had wormed her way into my heart, my head, and every pore in me.

Stretching my neck one way then the other, I crossed the shiny tiled floor of the reception area to the other hallway then walked back. "I'm fine."

Keep telling yourself that.

Taylor closed the distance between us. "What are you doing here, Josh?"

Candace joined our circle. "Riley was taken by Mr. Gansett. I thought you had been too." She sighed.

I felt closed in as the ladies had me somewhat pinned against the reception desk. "You don't have to be this close. Just make sure you're on my right side."

They didn't move.

Charlie panted as he sat next to me.

Taylor shoved her hands into the pockets of her ankle-length jeans. "I know Mr. Gansett has Riley, as do the two men from Boston who showed up here last week."

My eyebrows vanished into my hairline. "How do you know?"

I concentrated on her lips, willing them to move.

"Josh, I don't want you to freak out. I know you and Riley don't trust me. But what I did, I did because of loyalty."

My jaw hardened to stone. So many interrogation techniques that I'd used as a SEAL flickered in front of me. I swore if she said she was working for Gansett or Moretti or both, I would consider using any one of those painful methods to get her to talk.

"Either talk, or I'll make you," I said in a voice that didn't sound like mine.

Taylor's throat bobbed as she produced a green thumb drive from her pocket.

Candace, who was still rather close to me, squeaked like one of Charlie's dog toys.

I stalked the short distance and snagged the darn thing from Taylor. "So this is why Riley was taken?" I got out my phone to call Agent Wallace.

Taylor grabbed my wrist. "Don't call the cops."

"I'm not," I snapped. "I'm calling the FBI."

"Then Riley will die." Taylor didn't mince words.

I snarled so loud, it echoed, even though my heart had stopped altogether.

Taylor didn't back down. "Liza called me. She's meeting me

here in less than two hours. So is Mr. Gansett and those two thugs from Boston."

That earlier fear Candace had had written all over her face returned. "Maybe I should go."

Charlie pushed his way in between Taylor and me. He was always in tune to tension.

Taylor pursed her lips. "Please, Josh. All they want is the drive, then they'll let Riley go."

After rounding the desk, I stuck the thumb drive into the computer. I was curious what was so important that it could cost Riley or Liza her life. "Candace, please do me one thing, then you can go. Unlock your computer."

She did as I asked.

"While she gets the files up on the screen," I said to Taylor, "tell me everything." We had time, but I had to think fast.

I suspected that Moretti's men and Mr. Gansett would show up before Liza to corner her somehow.

Tap. Tap. Tap. Candace's fingers flew over the keys.

A thousand questions were flashing through my mind, but I decided to wait until Taylor told me her side of the story.

Taylor petted Charlie's head. "I was truthful about everything I told you and Riley. I just left some things out because Liza asked me to."

"Taylor, what Liza's involved in is dangerous. The mafia is not an organization you want to tango with." I planned on giving Liza a piece of my mind for sure.

Taylor hugged herself. "Liza needed my help, and no matter the danger, I didn't care. Still don't. My miserable world is messed up as it is. So putting my life on the line is a risk I'm willing to take, especially for a friend and a lady I admire tremendously."

I remembered Agent Wallace saying she had daddy issues. Maybe she wanted to prove how tough she was to her father. Still, part of me admired her for her strength, dedication, and staunch decision to help a friend. Those were all qualities of someone I would go into battle with. I respected her more in that moment than I had since I'd met her.

"How did you end up with the thumb drive and not Liza? And where is my cousin?"

Taylor tugged at a gold chain around her neck. "To make a long story short, Liza was in a rush when Haley unexpectedly came into town. She meant to grab the drive before she left the office last Thursday. Anyway, Liza was about to tell me where it was when Riley showed up. Fast-forward to an hour after I was fired. I came back to plead with Mr. Gansett to keep my job when I heard him talking on the phone. He mentioned Liza's name and said he'd checked her office for the thumb drive. So I went back to her office and found it."

"Why is Mr. Gansett involved in all this?" Candace asked. "He seems like a nice man. Scary when he's about to fire me."

I skirted around the desk. "Is the computer ready?"

"Sorry. I didn't want to interrupt. But the files are loaded."

Taylor and I settled behind Candace as she clicked on the first file. A picture emerged.

It took me a moment to zero in on what I was seeing.

Candace pushed her chair back, practically running over my foot. "That's the guy who was here today."

A bald man with a goatee was pointing a gun at a short, chubby man, who was lying on the ground with a blood-soaked shirt.

"He's one of the thugs," Taylor added.

I gripped the back of Candace's chair. "Agent Wallace is looking for him."

Candace bobbed her head. "You should call Agent Wallace. Get him over here before anyone shows up."

She was so right. We didn't stand a chance against mafia men who had guns and other weapons, who had a take-no-prisoner attitude, and who dealt with situations by killing people.

I wished I were in fighting shape, and I wished I had my tactical gear. I wished Charlie wasn't there. I didn't want him to get hurt. Man, I wished for a lot of things, particularly that Riley was safe.

I had my phone out, ready to tap on Agent Wallace's number.

"Josh, don't. Please," Taylor said. "Do you want to lose Riley? I know you don't. I saw how you looked at her."

I pushed my tongue against my teeth for no other reason than to not scream at Taylor. Then I sucked in air and paced, threading my fingers through my hair.

Charlie was on his feet, ready to leap into action, much like he'd done when I'd been pacing the doctor's office, waiting on the doctor to tell Dad and me what his diagnosis was.

"Did Liza say what the plan was? In fact, call her," I demanded.

Taylor came up to me, stared me in the eyes, and said, "You need to calm down. I'm going to put the thumb drive in Candace's desk drawer. Then all of us are going to leave."

I swallowed hard. "I'm not leaving. I suggest both of you leave." I pulled out my car keys. "Taylor, take Charlie. My truck is on the third floor of the parking garage across the street. It's a Toyota Tundra, dark blue. The GPS has the directions to the Redwood Cove Inn. Go there and give Charlie to Drake."

Taylor reared back. "You can't stay here by yourself. You can hardly hear. You need someone to have your back."

I laughed, mainly because she was right, especially if I wigged out like I had earlier. Then I was no good at helping anyone.

I glanced down the opposite hallway. Suddenly, I had an idea.

23

RILEY

The streets of San Francisco had construction zones everywhere. After we'd hung up with Liza, I'd wondered what in the world we would do for two hours before we met with her. My question was answered as we sat at light after light or had to backtrack because Leo, who wasn't from California, had no clue where he was going, especially when construction took us out of our way.

Mr. Gansett tried to tell him, but it was useless for anyone to give Leo orders. All he'd done was tell his uncle to pound sand in so many words.

"You seemed like a nice guy." I broke the silence, directing my words at Mr. Gansett. "Was all that a show when you fired Taylor and called the lady in London to see if Liza had been there?"

He quickly regarded the men in the seats, as though he didn't want them to hear his answer. "I'd been wanting to fire Taylor for over a month. The woman is useless. But Liza convinced me that Taylor needed saving. She's a rich girl with family problems that got in the way of her work. As far as the call to Ms. Norton, that wasn't exactly a show. I didn't know where Liza was. I believed Taylor did. I was getting close to finding Liza until these two yahoos showed up and ruined things."

Leo turned right onto another busy street. "You were far from close, Uncle. We had to do something."

"All you want is to see your lost love," Mr. Gansett fired back. "Bart's right. Your father will have your head on a platter if we don't get that drive back."

I squirmed. My backside was numb. My attempt at freeing my hands had failed. To make matters worse, the air in the van was becoming more rancid, as if someone had bathed in a bag of onions.

"Did you know Liza had the thumb drive?" I asked.

Mr. Gansett braced his elbows on his knees as the van bounced over a bump. "I overheard her on the phone telling someone she had a thumb drive with evidence that could put Moretti away for a long time."

"How does Haley fit into this mess?"

Mr. Gansett stabbed a thumb at Bart. "She saw this yahoo kill someone."

I gulped down air as I thought of another nagging question. "Did you know who Liza was when you hired her?"

He dipped his head as he swung his gaze to the front. "My nephew wanted to find Liza a job. He also wanted to keep her close for many reasons."

"My father," Leo chimed in, "doesn't trust easily. He wanted to keep an eye on those who quit after the raid, especially one I slept with. I also wanted her to be happy."

Oh my. He was in love with Liza. I knew that whatever happened, Leo would protect Liza and maybe me, and for that, some of my panic waned.

After several turns and two more stoplights, we were entering the garage underneath Stitches Inc. My stomach began to spin out of control.

Mr. Gansett seemed deep in thought. Maybe he was planning his next move that had nothing to do with Leo and Bart's objective.

Nevertheless, three men against Liza wasn't going to end well. Then, in pure Riley fashion, I thought the worst. What if Liza didn't show? What if they didn't get the thumb drive? What if I died tonight?

Hairs shot straight up on my arms as if I'd touched a live electrical wire. I breathed deeply through my nose, doing everything I could not to panic to the point I would pass out. I had never been known to do that, but I'd never been kidnapped before.

Then my pulse slowed as if a hard wind blew and took with it the terror hijacking my body. Josh was in the city. Josh would save the day.

The man can't hear. He limps too. "So what?" I silently shouted. Josh would protect those he loves. *He doesn't love you.* Okay, he would protect his friends or friends of loved ones. *Stop torturing yourself, Riley.*

I had to love my subconscious.

A phone somewhere up front dinged. Bart glanced down in his lap. I couldn't tell if he was looking at my phone or his.

Mr. Gansett wiped the sweat off his brow. "Park in the spot closest to the door. I'd rather not call attention to us."

Bart produced a gun out of the glove compartment. I was officially about to pee in my nice lacy underwear.

A car's tires squealed on the cement floor of the garage.

Liza immediately came to mind. Or maybe it was Josh. It didn't matter. Whoever was out there would help.

Silence filled every corner of the van. Until…

"Hellllllp!" I screamed at the top of my lungs.

Bart whirled around in his seat, aiming a rather large gun at me. "Shut up. Or I'll make sure you never scream again.

Mr. Gansett practically dove at me and covered my mouth. I kicked, wiggled, and kicked again, flopping around like a fish out of water.

Lowering his gun, Bart swiveled in his seat. "Is that Liza?"

I choked as my lungs burned for air.

"No," Leo said. "The truck left."

Mr. Gansett removed his hand.

I took deep breaths, realizing the onion man was none other than Mr. Gansett.

I didn't get a chance to do much else before Mr. Gansett untied my ankles. "Let's get this over with."

Before I could take a breath, I was being dragged out of the van and into the elevator with a gun to my back. My nerves were singing in tune with my pulse.

Bart pushed the barrel of the gun into me. "Try any slick moves, and I'll use this."

I had no doubt he would.

As the elevator ascended, I stuck out my chin for nothing more than to show these men I wasn't afraid. Yet my insides were knotted to the point that my stomach hurt. I wanted nothing more than to be home on the couch, watching a Red Sox game with Ross. Better yet, lounging on the porch behind Redwood Cove Inn, listening to the waves crash against the shore while I drank a lemonade with Josh next to me.

None of that was in my future, not when the mafia had me in their grasp and the only way out of this situation was in a body bag. Sure, they'd been accommodating in the van, talking to me as if we were old friends, but that was only a façade.

Tell her everything because in the end, she won't be around to tell the feds anything.

The elevator dinged, and my heart plummeted.

When the doors slid open, fear so darned strong gripped me from every angle. Mr. Gansett and Leo walked out.

Bart tried to pull me with him, but I didn't move. Something told me not to step out. If I did, I wouldn't see the light of day ever again.

Bart got behind me just before the doors slid shut. "I'm warning you." He pressed the open door button as he kept the gun trained on me. Then he released the button and shoved me out before the doors could close.

Jerk came to mind as I stumbled. With my hands tied behind my back, I had no way to catch myself. The floor rose up fast, and I landed on my face. A sharp and excruciating pain radiated outward.

Leo helped me up, and when we locked eyes, he winced.

I couldn't help but do the same for a vastly different reason—pain.

Bart jabbed the gun into me. "Move." His tone could've split a glacier in two.

Blood oozed out of my nose and slid into my mouth, the metallic taste exploding on my tongue. The urge to spit was overpowering, but my reflex kicked in as Bart pushed me, making me swallow.

Before long, a familiar area came into view. We were on the opposite end of Mr. Gansett's office, looking down at the reception desk that was illuminated by the fluorescent lights above. The word "creepy" came to mind, giving me the sense that I was in a horror movie. The closed doors on both sides of the hall reminded me of that long hallway in *The Shining.* When Leo and Mr. Gansett stopped cold, I squealed.

Bart abandoned me, barreling through the two men like a bowling ball.

This was my chance to run, get away, seek freedom. But then I caught sight of a petite figure standing in the distance like an angel who had come to rescue me. I wasn't exaggerating. With the light from above, the woman looked as if she had a halo over her brown hair that was draped around her shoulders.

The pain in my face diminished. The nausea that was slowly creeping north ebbed. I blinked several times. Suddenly, Liza became crystal clear. My excitement was at an all-time high. Finally, I was laying eyes on my best friend.

"Liza?" I shouted at the top of my lungs. "Is that you?"

For a second, I thought she was happy to see me. But her gaze was riveted on Leo, who had his mouth slightly ajar. So much love was pouring off him despite the fact that she had something of value that could imprison his father for life.

Nevertheless, she was still my best friend. I was over the moon to see her even if her smile wasn't for me.

She held up the thumb drive. "Send Riley down here." She had that confident tone again, the same one I'd never heard from her before that day. She didn't have an ounce of shakiness or a cracked voice or anything.

You're not doing so bad yourself. I begged to differ. I couldn't save myself if my life depended on it. *You gave it a try when you kneed Leo in the groin.*

Leo growled or maybe moaned.

Bart marched down toward Liza.

I held my breath, checking over my shoulder. This was my chance to save myself.

Leo gripped my arm with a vise-like grip. "I might be in love with your friend, but I'm not an idiot."

"If you love her that much, you'll let me go," I said.

Bart was halfway to Liza with the gun pointed at her. "Either you throw that drive to me, or you'll get a bullet to the head."

As if Bart had said the magic line, all hell broke loose.

24

______

JOSH

Taylor and I were in one of the many abandoned offices on the other end of where Liza's office was located. I'd been pacing and talking to myself, praying that what was about to go down would happen without my cousin or Riley getting hurt. I was also antsy because I had no control, I had no weapon, and I had no way to help. The only thing I took comfort in was knowing that Charlie was safe with Candace. I'd had Candace take him before I'd called Agent Wallace.

I'd had no other choice but to bring in the cavalry despite Taylor's plea not to. I wanted to be a hero, to save the day, to save my cousin, and to rescue the woman I was falling hard for. But Taylor had reminded me I couldn't hear, and since I'd nearly blacked out when Taylor had shown up, I wasn't exactly the model hero I'd been when I was a SEAL. And for that, I had my fists clenched and my jaw locked tight, plus nerves were eating the lining of my stomach.

In addition, Agent Wallace had ordered me not to engage under any circumstances if the situation got out of control. He knew I wanted to help. He knew I was itching to strap on a gun and go into battle. Man, that was the understatement of the century.

Taylor chewed her nails as she kept her ear to the door. The only reason she was in the building was because we'd run out of time. As for me, there was no way I was leaving.

Taylor raised her finger to her lips, indicating that we needed to be quiet. My heart jackhammered against my ribs. Then she motioned to the door with her finger. "They're here," she mouthed.

I stopped pacing. I stopped breathing. I pressed my ear to the door, straining to hear a pin drop.

Suddenly, I heard Riley call out to Liza, which told me she had to be screaming. As if that were my cue to jump into action, I grabbed the doorknob.

Taylor shook her head vigorously, her eyes narrowed as she covered her hand over mine. "Wait," she mouthed.

I suppressed a growl. Patience wasn't my strong suit. Besides, I'd been trained to attack at the right moment, and that was the right moment. Riley needed me.

As hard as it was, I held steady, again my ear and the door becoming one. I heard a muffled voice, then a man's voice became deeper and sharper. "You'll get a bullet to the head."

I didn't need to hear anything else. I threw open the door and tackled the big guy to the ground. His bald head slammed against the wall, and his gun slid out of his grasp. I wrestled with him, but he got me in a choke hold with my back to his front.

My lungs screamed for air. I slammed my head into his nose. He faltered, and his grip on me loosened. I shrugged out of his hold and primed my fist, ready to use the baldheaded guy as a punching bag, when someone from behind me caught my arm.

"We got it from here," Agent Wallace said loudly on my good side.

The dude snarled when Dennison appeared and took him into custody.

A muscle ticked in Agent Wallace's jaw. "I thought I told you not to engage."

"I've been known not to obey," I returned. Luckily, for everyone, no guns went off.

But agents, guns, and bad guys faded as I searched up and down the hall for only one woman. My pulse was still beating rapidly, but now for a vastly different reason. I didn't want to see Mr. Gansett or Moretti's son being escorted out in handcuffs.

Riley's cherry blossom scent wafted in the air, and every muscle in me tightened and loosened at the same time. My heart beat like a wild horse running through the vast open plains.

In slow motion, I pivoted on my heel and looked behind me. When I did, I lost my breath—not because of her smile and not because she was alive, but her gray eyes had a storm brewing in them of epic proportions. Or maybe it just looked that way since the underside of her eyes were turning black and blue. My gaze traveled down to find blood smeared around her nose.

I rushed to her, wanting nothing more than to lift her in my arms and take care of her. Yet the moment we were face to face, all sense of where I was disappeared. I cupped her cheek, breathed her in, and slowly lowered my lips to hers.

She sucked in a sharp breath and nodded as if to say, "Please kiss me."

So I did. I kissed her as if she were my last breath. In that moment, I knew I didn't want this woman to leave California. I also knew that I would do anything to make sure she didn't.

Our tongues collided in a heated kiss as she pressed her body to mine. I kept one hand on her soft cheek and snaked my other hand around to her lower back to make sure she didn't fall, leave, or back away.

She abandoned my mouth. "I want that dinner and a movie."

I lifted her up in my arms. "And I want you."

All was right in the world.

25

RILEY

Puffy clouds hung over the Pacific Ocean far in the distance. Liza and I sat on a couch swing on the back porch of the Redwood Cove Inn. One day had passed since Josh had saved me. If it weren't for him, Liza and I might not be alive. Sure, the federal agents were waiting for the right moment to storm out of the offices, but Bart had been a second away from using his gun on either me or Liza or both of us. Plus, Josh had had the fortitude to alert Agent Wallace despite Taylor following Liza's orders not to bring in the cops.

I moved Liza's long hair out of the way and laid my head on her shoulder. "I'm still mad at you. And I have a ton of questions."

Agent Wallace had questioned Liza without anyone but other agents present.

"Let's wait for my cousin. I know he's chomping at the bit to ask me the same questions you have, and I would prefer to only answer them once, especially after being interrogated until four in the morning."

I could do that. I didn't blame her either. Having to relive the ordeal over and over again would've been maddening. I knew I would have to answer Ross's questions, but he wouldn't be as nice as Josh, especially when he saw my black eyes.

"While we wait, let's talk about Leo. I'm sure Josh doesn't want to hear about him."

She tensed. "Nothing to say about Leo."

I sat up. "He's in love with you. The man confessed as much."

She whipped her head at me, her brown eyes full of despair. "He and I could never be. I don't agree with his morals or what he and his family do for a living. I made a mistake sleeping with him."

"How come you never told me?"

Waves crashed on the shore.

Her foot moved back and forth. "Would you have approved?"

"Whether I would have or not, I am your friend, and you know I don't judge. I would've supported you no matter what." I wouldn't have approved, but love was a funny animal. I believed love found a person, not the other way around.

She patted my thigh. "Thank you. I do care for Leo, but not enough to live his lifestyle. So when are you leaving for Boston?"

I didn't want to leave. I wanted to spend time with Liza, and I wanted to go on that date with Josh. I'd told him I would, but the wedding I had next weekend required me to be in Boston. When I'd spoken to my assistant that morning, she had told me the bride-to-be wanted a refund if I didn't show. I couldn't say I blamed the young woman. I had promised her that I would be with her every step of the way. I also had the mayor's daughter's wedding coming up, and I had so much to do.

"Tomorrow."

"Josh will be sad," Liza said. "When I told him to take care of you, I didn't mean to fall in love." She giggled.

"He's not in love with me."

"Pfft. He is. I know my cousin. I have never seen him head over heels for someone. That kiss yesterday? That reunion between you two? Wow."

Heat pinched my cheeks. "He certainly knows how to kiss." I touched my lips. "I will be sad too. I promised him a date."

"Oh, he'll hold you to that promise."

"Long-distance relationships don't really work," I said, more to myself.

"I'll make sure this one does." Out of nowhere, a tear slid down her cheek. "I can't tell you how sorry I am that I put you in danger. That was never my intention."

I reached over and grasped her hand. "You didn't force me to do anything. You didn't even force Taylor. That woman admires you so much, although I had my doubts about her at first."

"She's a great person. Her father cut off her inheritance because she didn't want to go to business school, and she wants nothing to do with her family's winery or any of their businesses. She's going to be a great fashion designer."

"She's also getting married. Right?"

"I think her relationship with her fiancé is strained because her father disowned her. So we'll see."

I'd seen many couples break up midway through the wedding planning stages for many reasons.

We swung on the couch swing, the movement soothing. I could sit there all day, thinking, reading, working, and watching the ocean in all its glory. As the surfers paddled out to catch the next big wave, I had an idea.

I let go of Liza's hand. "We've talked about opening up a dress shop, and I was thinking that maybe we could do that sooner rather than later. There's a bridal shop in town for sale. What if we bought it? You could get things up and running, and I can come out a few times a year and help. You could hire Taylor."

The swing stopped. "Seriously?"

"I have money in the bank, and you don't have a job."

Mr. Gansett had been arrested, so the company was in disarray, and I didn't think Liza was going back to Stitches Inc. I knew Taylor wasn't. Even if Mr. Gansett kept the company running, he thought she wasn't talented.

Liza curled strands of her hair behind her ear, her eyes glistening as she smiled. "On one condition. You move out here."

I choked. Boston was my home. I had Ross and Mom. I had

several friends as well, but none as close as Liza. I also had my own business to run. I couldn't just give that up.

"Josh wants you here. I do too. I hear Josh's dad adores you. Plus, you're the one with the business acumen. I draw and sketch. You plan and organize and make things happen."

That was the first time I'd seen her so happy. Even when she'd left Boston, she hadn't been that happy. Granted, we'd been saying goodbye to each other at the time.

The door squeaked open, and Charlie came out, wagging his tail. A second later, Josh swaggered out wearing jeans low on his hips and a Navy SEAL T-shirt stretched across his toned chest. His green gaze zeroed in on me.

My heart went haywire. Maybe that was a sign that I should say yes to Liza and move out to California.

26

JOSH

Charlie immediately went over to Riley. I was afraid his heart would break the minute she got on that plane the next day. I leaned against the porch rail and swung my gaze from Riley to Liza and back to Riley. It gutted me to see her beautiful face marred with black eyes. After our epic kiss, she'd told me that Bart had pushed her out of the elevator. It was all I could do to restrain myself from hunting him down. But he would get what was due to him in prison.

The soothing sound of the waves ebbing and flowing behind me did nothing to calm the butterflies in my stomach. Despite her black eyes, Riley was still gorgeous. Her hair was up in a messy bun, and her long, smooth neck was on display. I puffed out my cheeks for no other reason than to calm my body down, but that was impossible.

I swept my gaze down to her cute painted toes that were peeking through a pair of sandals. I itched to rub her feet. Some people weren't into feet, but I was. That was the one physical attribute I noticed first if a woman was wearing sandals like Riley.

But before I got Riley alone, which was on my list considering she was leaving tomorrow, I had to get in all the kisses and make-out sessions I could.

First, though, I had questions for my cousin, who appeared tired with dark circles beneath her eyes. In one sense, I wanted to yell at her, and in the other, I knew she'd done what she thought was right. If I were being honest, I would've done the same as her and hid until I could come up with a plan.

Liza sighed. "I'll start since I know, cousin, your curiosity is killing you."

She knew me well.

I crossed my arms over my chest and settled in. Charlie lay at Riley's feet, and Riley held one of her nails hostage between her teeth.

"Shortly before the raid on Moretti's company last year, I found several photos and documents on the company's server," Liza began. "I'd been searching for a folder with some old fashion designs and just happened to click on a folder that was titled 'Milan.' My predecessor had organized a fashion show in Milan, so I thought I could get ideas from old designs and turn them into current trends. Only the folder had photos of—"

"Bart killing someone," I said.

Both Riley and Liza's noses scrunched.

I ground my teeth together. "I saw everything on that drive."

Liza shuddered. "Don't say that too loud. Anyway, the folder had a ton of incriminating evidence, and it bothered me for weeks. I thought of quitting well before the raid. I thought of sending all the information to the police, but I didn't want to end up dead. Then three days before the raid, I overheard Stefano talking to one of his men about the feds and how they might be paying them a visit. Stefano ordered his man to wipe the computers clean. I should've just left and not looked back. Instead, I copied that folder onto a thumb drive."

She glanced out at the ocean. "I considered giving the drive to Agent Wallace the day of the raid when he questioned me. But I wasn't ready to deal with running for the rest of my life. Then Stefano was arrested recently. I thought maybe it was time I hand over the evidence to Agent Wallace. That way, Stefano would go to prison for a very long time. I called Agent Wallace, but I never heard back. Then out of the blue, Haley called me. She'd been working late one night and saw Bart killing a man in the warehouse. She knew she couldn't go to the cops. She knew they would kill her, and she didn't know who to turn to."

"So she came out here. Why?" I asked. "I get that she's your friend, but you couldn't protect her." But I understood her wanting to get out of town.

"I told her to track down Agent Wallace, which was another reason I called him. But then she showed up in my office the day Riley flew in, the same day Bart and Leo stopped by too. I had to help her. At that point, I didn't have time to do much else. I even forgot to grab the thumb drive from my office. I did plan on meeting Riley that day, but then Bart and Leo were following me. I called Taylor, and without going into detail, asked if I could lay low at one of her family's abandoned wineries. I told her to keep her phone handy, and I shut mine off since Leo kept calling me."

"How did they know you had it?" I asked.

"Mr. Gansett," Riley said. "He told me he overheard Liza talking about it on the phone."

Liza picked at a nail. "I'm still miffed that I missed the connection between Mr. Gansett and the Moretti family. He was always kind to me. He was a good boss. But thinking back to when I interviewed with him, he was the only one not to care about my former employer. I guess that should've been a neon sign."

"They wanted to keep an eye on you," Riley mumbled.

"Need I say you should've gotten me involved?" I said more than asked.

"I tried to keep everyone out of danger. That didn't work, of course." She frowned at Riley, then looked at me. "I definitely didn't want the mafia to storm into Redwood Cove Inn. You nor your dad needed that kind of trouble. Besides"—she smiled—"you would've gone all Navy SEAL on them."

I smirked. "That would've been okay. I miss the heck out of my days as a SEAL."

Liza came over to me and pressed a hand to my chest. "Josh, I love you to death. You've been through enough." She gave me a hug. "Now it's time you get the girl," she whispered in my ear. Then she pulled away. "Riley is talking about buying that bridal shop down the street. Maybe you can convince her to move out here." She and Riley exchanged an unspoken message. Then she went over to the door. "Charlie, come on. Let's go see Drake."

Charlie popped up and disappeared with Liza inside the inn.

My tongue was tied, or maybe Riley had me under one of her spells with the way she was looking at me as though I were her world. Man, I wanted to be her everything. "Is that true?"

She shied away. "Maybe."

"You do owe me a date."

"And you owe me another heart-stopping kiss. I think that might convince me," she teased.

Whether she was teasing or not, I didn't think; I only reacted.

I helped her to her feet and peppered kisses along her neck until our lips were fused together. Then I kissed her like a man possessed.

My dad had predicted we would be married within two years, and whether or not we would, I knew I would marry Riley Lewis one day.

EPILOGUE
RILEY

"Ouch," Liza cried. "I will never get used to being a human pin cushion."

I giggled as I watched Liza fit a wedding dress she'd designed on a beautiful young bride with golden locks who was glowing with happiness. That was the part of the wedding industry that I loved the most: seeing brides glow and cry with joy.

Taylor rushed out of the backroom, bubbly and full of energy. "I can't find the lace you were talking about, Liza." When she spotted me, she waved. "Riley, so good to see you."

I hadn't had a chance to see Taylor since I'd arrived in town three days ago. She seemed to have gained some weight, and she'd cut her long blond tresses. The bob-style cut suited her.

Six long months had passed since I was kidnapped, and three months had gone by since Liza and Haley had testified at Stefano's trial. He had been convicted and was spending many years behind bars. Bart had been sent to prison with no chance of parole. He'd gotten a worse sentence than Stefano since he'd committed murder. As for Leo, he had been slapped with a short sentence for kidnapping me, as had Mr. Gansett.

Haley had gone into hiding. I'd never gotten a chance to meet her and probably never would. Liza had told me that Haley had left the country and no one would ever find her.

"Take a break," Liza said to the bride.

The shop was set up with refreshments for waiting guests of our clients. The bride-to-be pulled out her phone as Taylor poured her a glass of water.

Liza came over to me, her hair up in a ponytail. "Hey, bestie." She kissed me on the cheek. "Where have you been?"

"On the phone with my assistant all morning." I'd recently sold my wedding business in Boston to one of my assistants. "I was also trying to find an apartment in town, and I had to sign more papers for this place." I'd bought the bridal shop four months ago, and one week ago, I had packed up and moved from Boston to California.

Liza crossed her arms over her chest, angling her head. "You'll stay with me. I told you that."

"You mean stay with Josh and his dad." I would've loved to do that, but with Liza living with them, I was afraid the house might be too crowded.

She huffed. "They want you to stay there."

I knew that, but if Josh and I were going to build our relationship, which we kind of had been via phone for six months, I wanted a little space to breathe sometimes.

Rather than hash it out with Liza, I changed the subject. "So the sign people will be here today."

Her attitude shifted instantly. "I can't wait to see it."

I wasn't surprised. She'd been dying to get the name on the outside of the building. We'd decided on the name Hidden Gem. She'd suggested it because she thought every bride was a hidden gem. I couldn't have agreed more. Brides to me were special and, with my care, bloomed into beautiful flowers on their wedding days.

The bell on the door dinged.

I turned to find the man who made my insides all giddy walking in with an ear-to-ear grin and eyes only for me. My chest rose and fell the closer he came, and when his arms went around my waist, I melted into a puddle of mush.

"It's time for our dinner date," he said in a husky tone.

I reached up on my toes and whispered in his right ear, which was a habit now. "Let's skip dinner and take a walk on the beach." I wasn't hungry anyway.

"Anywhere you are, I'm there. The beach sounds perfect." His hot breath on my neck gave me goose bumps.

We said goodbye to Liza and Taylor and made our way down to the beach through a public entrance not far from the Hidden Gem.

By the time we dug our toes in the sand, the bright-orange sun was sliding down on the horizon.

Josh interlaced his fingers with mine as we walked along the edge of the frigid water. The breeze was in our faces, and the sounds of the ocean played a soft tune.

We were close to the cliffs behind his house when he came to an abrupt halt.

"What's wrong?" I asked.

His hard gaze roamed over me. Normally, I would blush and shy away at the way he was looking at me, but if I were reading him correctly, he had something to tell me.

"Is your dad okay?" I asked. *Please say yes.* In one of our many conversations, he'd told me that his dad's ALS hadn't gotten worse. Maybe something had changed in the last month, although I didn't think so since I'd seen his dad only yesterday. He had seemed as happy as he'd been the morning I met him.

Josh nodded, his eyes shifting back and forth. "I need to tell you something."

I brought my finger up to my mouth and bit my nail.

He grinned. "It's not that bad."

I slapped a hand to my heart in an attempt to slow it down. "Josh Bandon, if you don't tell me right now, I will throw you in the ocean."

He let out a belly laugh "Baby doll, you couldn't if you tried."

I raised an eyebrow. "Is that a challenge?" I was up for a challenge but maybe not at that moment. The Pacific was cold even on a warm day.

His fingers danced in my hair. "The last time I was in love with a girl was in high school. Since then, I haven't gotten serious with anyone, mainly because of my SEAL days. And the past six months have been excruciatingly painful with you in Boston and me here. We've talked a lot on the phone, and during those phone calls, I've always been dying to tell you one thing, but I didn't want to over the phone. What I have to say can only be said face to face."

"That you love me?" I asked, my pulse galloping a mile a minute.

He lost his smile. "No."

My heart fell to the sand, and if I weren't mistaken, the retreating wave took my heart with it. One of the reasons I'd chosen to move over three thousand miles was Josh. If I'd read him wrong, then boy, I needed some serious help.

His slow grin parted into the most belly-tingling smile. "I'm in love with you. There's a difference."

I punched him playfully on one of his tattooed and muscled arms. "Semantics. And for that, I should dunk you in the ocean."

As if the sea had heard me, a wave crashed to shore, knocking me over, and before I could do anything, the undertow was taking me with it. Water filled my mouth as I took in a breath. I could swim, but the undertow was strong. I bobbed to the surface, choking, when a hand grabbed my foot.

The wave receded, allowing Josh to get a better grip on me before he lifted me in his arms. "I got you, baby doll."

I locked my hands around his neck as the ice-cold water seeped into my pores.

He carried me a good distance from the ocean's edge then set me down on dry sand, then rubbed my arms, my head, and my legs. "Are you okay?"

I laughed. "You saved me once again."

"I'll always save you, Riley. I'm so darn in love with you, I can't eat. I can't sleep, and if you don't marry me, I might die."

I spit sandy water out of my mouth. "Wait. What?"

"I'm asking you to marry me." He locked eyes with me as water dripped from his hair onto my face.

If I were still cold, I didn't feel a thing. I'd planned to tell Josh how I felt, but I'd never expected a marriage proposal.

I lifted my head and pressed my lips to his. I wanted a future with him. Actually, I wanted forever with him. "Yes, I will marry you. I'm hopelessly in love with you."

We rolled around in the sand, laughing, kissing, and laughing some more. It wasn't the way I'd expected to be proposed to after falling into the ocean, but I would never forget this day.

The end.

Thank you for reading Riley and Josh's story. For another romantic suspense by S.B. Alexander check out Hart of Darkness here: https://sbalexanderbooks.com/pages/hart-series

ABOUT THE AUTHOR

Award-winning author **S.B. Alexander** writes sports and paranormal romances and heart-pounding romantic suspense. Dive into her character-driven romances and meet the hot heroes and feisty heroines who steam up the pages of every book with all the feels, family drama, a sprinkle of action, and a dash of intrigue as they embark on their happily ever afters.

S.B., or Susan as she likes to be called, is a Navy veteran, former high school teacher, and corporate sales executive. She loves sports, especially baseball, although nowadays, you can find her on the golf course, swinging for that elusive hole-in-one.

Her motto: "Life is too short to waste. So live every moment like it's your last."

You can connect with S.B. Alexander in the following ways:
Reader Group: http://sbalexander.com/sbareaderroom
Author Website: https://sbalexander.com
Buy direct from the author: https://sbalexanderbooks.com
Newsletter: https://sbalexander.com/newsletter
Email: susan@sbalexander.com

facebook.com/sbalexander.authorpage

instagram.com/sbalexanderauthor

pinterest.com/sbalexander0046

tiktok.com/@susanbalexander

ALSO BY S.B. ALEXANDER

THE MAXWELL SERIES

New Adult Contemporary Romance

Dare to Kiss

Dare to Dream

Dare to Love

Dare to Dance

Dare to Live

Dare to Breathe

Dare to Embrace

The Kade & Lacey Collection Boxset

THE VAMPIRE NAVY SEAL: SAM & LAYLA

Paranormal Romance

The Hunted

The Predator

The Union

The Dawning

The Prodigies

The Prophecy

The Rebirth

Sam & Layla Box Set 1-3

THE MAXWELL FAMILY SAGA SERIES

Young Adult Sweet Contemporary Romance

My Heart to Touch

My Heart to Hold

My Heart to Give

My Heart to Keep

Maiken & Quinn Collection

STANDALONES

New Adult Contemporary Romance

Crazy For You

Unforgettable

Breaking Rules

Rescuing Riley

Holding On To Forever

THE HART SERIES

Romantic Suspense

Hart of Darkness

Hart of Vengeance

Hart of Redemption

THE VAMPIRE SEAL SERIES: Jo & Webb

Young Adult Paranormal Romance

On the Edge of Humanity

On the Edge of Eternity

On the Edge of Destiny

On the Edge of Misery

On the Edge of Infinity

The Vampire Navy SEAL Collection

Visit https://sbalexander.com/all-books/ to learn more about S.B. Alexander books and future releases. Please note release dates are subject to change based on reader demand and the author's schedule. Subscribing to the author's newsletter or following her on Facebook is the best way to stay updated with planned new releases.